Encounter Uganda

Dr. Therone Wade

Ingram 5/22/08 91399

Copyright © 2007 by Dr. Therone Wade

Africa
Fic
Wade

Encounter Uganda
by Dr. Therone Wade

Printed in the United States of America

ISBN 978-1-60477-493-1

www.xulonpress.com

433 6306

This book is dedicated to
all the children of Uganda
in need of rescue.

ACKNOWLEDGEMENTS

I would like to thank my mother, who made the brave decision to complete her pregnancy with me in full, which was not the case for my older brother who sits with mom in heaven today. I would like to thank my mother-in-law Jackie for raising such an amazing daughter to become my wife. Also, I would like to thank my wife Precious (Lashona) whose sacrifice and prayers made each step of this ministry possible. She has truly been my Eve in the garden – minus the apple part. I would like to acknowledge Therone Jr. (my son) as well as Tyra and Daniece (my twin daughters) for their love and support in allowing their dad to be one for fellow brothers and sisters across the ocean.

I would like to thank Lisa and Doug Painter for editing this literary work. Additionally, thank you to my friends from various cultures and addresses in America and Africa for your support in person, on the phone, and via the Internet. Certainly, I would like to thank my fellow missionary friends currently living in South America, China, and Central Africa who have encouraged me through their lives.

Not least, not lost, and certainly not last, God for grace in allowing a flawed vessel to bring hope on His behalf to others.

FORWARD
By John Guest

D r. Therone Wade has written a very convincing and empathetic story about life in Uganda. Since I, myself, was one of those who initiated the Encounter Uganda Mission Team, (of which Therone Wade was a vital part), I can see that he has captured the mood of the spirit and life in Uganda, and the tensions that exist there. Being of African-American descent himself, Therone's commitment to the Continent of his forebears, and the extraordinary work that he did for the children of Uganda, adds further credibility to his character as an author, telling of experiences that are very true to life, and true to his passion.

I trust that Therone's writing will stir many, to be concerned and invested in the issues of a land, very distant from America. Africa has become "up close and real," because the world has, indeed, become a global village. With instant communication, visually as well as verbally, of calamities and opportunities in distant parts of the world, we enter into the anguish and dreams of other people! Their burdens, in some sense, become ours! So it was, with Dr. Therone Wade! So may it be with you!

PREFACE
By Lydia Wamani

Through this writing, God purposes to show His care about children in the world in regards to His kingdom. He further confirms Therone Wade's call and passion for Africa, particularly Uganda (Bunyoro). This has been manifest through his tireless efforts and of his counter parts in the struggle to evangelize children. I strongly believe that it has been through God's guidance and inspiration that Dr. Therone has come up with such a wonderful compilation, which I am sure will touch and transform many lives of those who will have the opportunity to read it.

Dr. Therone has been working as the team leader/ American coordinator for Encounter Uganda for many years. He has helped greatly in the training of children club leaders and Sunday school teachers in Bunyoro-Kitara Diocese and Maindi-Kitara Diocese. He has sacrificed his time and other resources to ensure that children are reached with the gospel. He has continually done this while in and outside the country. Over 200 teachers have been trained to help children know Christ. Also, over 30,000 thousand kids in schools, homes, and churches have been blessed through Dr. Therone's ministry. His vision is that all children in Africa be reached with the gospel of Christ. He has devoted his time to learn the African culture and the languages of the people in whom ENK-U operates. The time, interaction, and experience in Uganda have exposed him to all circles of life in Uganda. I am not afraid to say that Therone writes as a Ugandan. I do therefore commend this book for you who share in the passion and call to help the children on the continent of Africa know the Lord.

L ife is like a road we travel. No one knows how long he or she will be on this road. Some venture this road for copious years. Others' journey is short lived. Even more sadly, some voluntarily remove themselves. While hiking this road, there will be tough hills to scale and rough terrain to traverse. Time may seem to move rapidly traveling down precipitous hills. Life may seem commonplace as you move through the level long stretches. While hiking on this road, you may not reach your intended destination; you may have to take an unexpected detour (some by choice, others by force). However, it is normal in everyone's journey. You will encounter forks in the road. Deciding which one to take may require wisdom, risk taking, or faith. You will have accidents, but you can recover.

On this road, you will face trials and tribulations. You will have to travel through the storms of life as well as surprisingly sunny days. Tough winds may blow, but you must stay anchored and steadfast. There is one element you will face on this road that will make your journey both wonderful and painful - people. While traveling this road, some will attempt to discourage, distract, disrespect, and dismantle you. In order to be successful on this road, you must find one who is: **F**aithful, **R**eal, **I**ntelligent, **E**mpathetic, **N**urturing, and **Dear**. Never try to travel another's road. Stay on the path set for you.

Seeking corruptible possessions and misguided short-cuts weigh you down. Helping others builds you up. Don't pray for the easy road, but that you may have the strength to endure until the end.

"**D**id you pack everything?" Precious asked from the kitchen. The sounds of her footsteps grew louder as she walked towards the gameroom. "Joshua?"

"Yes," I answered.

"I asked if you had everything you needed for your trip," she stated.

"I'm sure I probably neglected to secure everything in my bag," I responded. The day that I both feared and eagerly anticipated had finally come into fruition. My missionary trip to Uganda was at last before me.

As I packed my check-in luggage, which could not weigh more than 50 pounds, I reminisced on the various events that led me to agree to this journey. It was two summers ago. I was the Summer SONsation camp director at Christ Church in Pittsburgh. The entire week was a miracle. During this particular summer, it rained nearly everyday. Kennywood Amusement park reported a loss of revenue that year due to inclement weather. I was quite concerned in that the Summer SONsation registered hundreds of children to attend this primarily outdoor camp.

During the week of camp, it rained only one day for less than ten minutes. This occurred the second day of camp. Later that week, it rained twice at night. However, this did not affect the activities planned for the next camp day. As the coordinator, supervising activities on the property was one of the charges given to me by the church council members.

Gazing over the Kentucky blue grass that covered a large percentage of the campus, I viewed children climbing a rock wall that was erected alongside the rear parking lot. Not too far in the distance, Kevin used a hose to wet a home-made slide that was 30 yards of industrial plastic on which shampoo was strategically placed. The children screamed as they took a running start on to the slide down hill that safely guided them into a pool of cool water. Of course, Kevin was waiting with a blast of water from the hose for them just moments prior to their descent into the basin.

Looking at the children reminded me of my childhood in the housing projects of the Hill District. It did not take theatrics from adults or advanced video games played on a high definition television for us to know that we were having fun. In our neighborhood, there were two things we had a wealth of during those years – the desire to enjoy our summer vacation and plenty of time.

Later that very same day at camp, it became more humid. The June sun appeared to focus all of its intensity on my back. Suddenly, a flashpoint in my life occurred. I heard someone whispering my name. I turned around with my lips poised to answer. I suddenly realized that I was alone. The voice I heard did not come from someone on campus. It came from within – from deep within my innermost being. At the same time, I felt a warm sensation within my chest. It pulsated and hovered just behind my rib cage. It lasted only a few seconds. It was designed to capture my attention; it achieved its objective.

"Africa. You're going to Africa." That was it.

These words were spoken clearly to me. I could hear them within my mind's ear. At that exact moment, I felt an overwhelming love for a group of people who I had never met, nor built a relationship or bond. I felt a warm tear fall from my eye and fall over my cheek. Just as quickly as the experience happened, it dissipated. I wiped the single stream of moisture from my face. I guessed that it wasn't actually a tear, but probably sweat from my forehead. Possibly, it could have been condensation that escaped from beneath my bandana. I dismissed this experience. I went about my duties as the camp director for the remainder of the day.

The week of camp ended without any concerns. I did not give the previous day's experience much thought until Saturday evening in my home. I was reclining in my lounge chair and recalled the entire experience in my mind.

"Honey, what's wrong?" Precious asked.

"Why do you ask?" I replied.

"You have this puzzled look on your face. What are you thinking about?" she stated.

"Nothing really. Except that I just can't seem to understand the experience I had while at camp last week," I added.

"Experience. What experience? I thought you said camp went fine." she stated. "Yes. Yes, it did. But I had this strange experience when I was walking around the church grounds."

I explained the entire encounter I had in great detail. The entire time that I was talking, Precious never said a word. When I finished talking, she simply sat there.

"Precious, are you alright? Did you hear anything I just told you?" I asked.

A moment passed and then she spoke. "I felt that you would be going away somewhere. I just did not know where. I can hardly wait to tell everyone!" Precious said excitedly.

"Everyone. No, no. There is no need to tell anyone what happened. They'll think I'm strange or weird. Just let it go for now."

She immediately walked out the room and went directly to the bedroom. I could hear the distinctive tones made on the cordless telephone when someone is dialing a phone number. Either she had to make an urgent call that she neglected to do earlier that day, or she was calling her mother. That one phone call to Nana, as the twins called her, would be the first of many calls on a phone chain strong enough to lift a Boeing 767-300 jet off the tarmac.

The next day, we would go to church. I assumed others would confront me about my experience. I prophesied that before the prayer of confession was over and done with, Pastor John, ushers, half the choir, and Deacon Simms would have heard about my experience at least twice. I would have to tell everyone that my wife was "going through a change" and her doctor was aware of the situation. I rather hated doing that to my wife behind her back as often as I did.

Weeks passed and even two seasons ended before any discussion regarding Africa occurred again. I was too busy working on my doctorate in higher education to yield my thoughts on peripheral topics or concerns. However, the subject matter of Africa had been resurrected. It arose again during the week of Easter in the commons area of the church on the lower level. The director of missions at the church, Lawrence Phillips, grabbed my arm as I was reaching for the wooden banister to walk up the steps.

"Good evening Joshua," Lawrence said with a wide smile.

I didn't mind lingering for a moment to talk with Lawrence. Actually, it was quite refreshing to hear him talk in his Australian accent. He came to the United States some time ago. He was a member of the church long before I joined. I turned around and found his hand extended.

"Hello Lawrence. Did you enjoy today's message?" I asked.

"Quite so," he quickly interjected. "I was wondering if you would be interested in joining the missionary team next year to Uganda."

Lawrence was never one to mince words. I supposed all that time on the outback takes a toll on one. Without allowing myself anytime to ponder my words, I responded immediately with excuses.

"I am working on my doctorate. I am deficient on money to take a trip to Atlanta to work with African-Americans, much less travel to Uganda to work with African-Africans. In fact, my bank statement does not provide a daily average balance. It merely has the words "INSUFFICIENT FUNDS" printed at the top in bold capital letters.

"Don't worry about it mate. We'll pay for everything. We've got it all covered.

I know that you can help lead a team in children's ministry," he continued. "It's a great opportunity to meet some very loving people. I believe that you'll find the experience one that you will never forget. This will be our sixth year working with the Bunyoro-Kitara Diocese in the region of Hoima."

As Lawrence talked, I thought about how it was less than 200 yards from that exact location that I was standing, where I had my surreal experience regarding Africa. Of course, I was very certain not to share my current thoughts with him at this time.

"Are you alright Joshua?"

"Yes. I just lost my focus for a second," I said.

Lawrence continued, "Think about it and give me a call this week at my office."

He pulled a wallet from his front pocket. He handed me a card. Lawrence walked up the stairs and eventually out of sight before I gathered my thoughts and headed for the minivan.

"What were you and Lawrence talking about?" Precious asked as I shut the door.

I swear that woman knows everything I do within a hundred miles. She was nowhere in sight during my entire conversation with Lawrence that I could see. This confirms my belief that her compact is actually a futuristic hand held communicator capable of inconceivable communication and surveillance unknown to today's current technology.

"Lawrence and I were not discussing anything too important."

"I believe he was saying something about you going with the missionary team to Uganda," she said.

Were my beliefs indeed true? "Precious, how did you know what he was talking to me about? You were nowhere in sight when Lawrence and I were downstairs. Where's your compact?" I asked.

Precious merely smiled widely and was silent for a moment. "I talked with Lawrence briefly in the lobby. He asked me where you were. I told him that you were probably downstairs speaking with Anton."

The drive home began in its typical manner. The twins and their brother were playing the Animal Moo Game in the second and third row seats. This was quite a simple game. I marveled that they enjoyed playing it for so long these many years. One person gives clues about a certain animal. The other players have to guess which animal the speaker is describing. It is a game Joshua Jr. invented on a family vacation to Niagara Falls.

"This animal lives on Dinosaur Island and goes 'roar-roar' real loud! Can you guess what it is?" Joshua Jr. asked.

Naomi responded quickly, "There is no such place as Dinosaur Island Jr. You're not playing the game correctly."

"It's a Tyrannosaurus rex!" Christa exclaimed. "Jr. likes that kind of dinosaur."

Naomi stated, "Mom, Christa and Jr. are not playing the game correctly."

"It's alright Naomi," Precious said. "If Jr. wants to describe dinosaurs, it's alright. They are animals too."

"Yeah!" Jr. blurted excitedly.

"Your father and I have something to discuss," Precious said. "Don't we honey?"

I did not respond. Precious knew that when I was not talking much, it usually meant I was in deep thought. It was at these times that she knew it was best to simply let me think through whatever I was reflecting on at that moment. I was grateful that she had grown to understand me.

It would appear that the handwriting was already on the wall regarding this mission journey to Africa. As wise people increase in age, they learn that experiences in life give them wisdom. Additionally, these same persons know that everything occurs for a purpose. There are no random events in life. This includes all the incidents surrounding one's birth. The parents, place, and date of birth for each child that breaks the membrane of the mother were ordained and divinely set.

This includes those persons who are artificially inseminated and those whose labors are induced. These, as well as other situations, may appear to be from the human rational that man orchestrated all of them. One may deduce that they were independent of divine intervention. However, an omniscient God knows all the actions and reactions to every event that occurs in the lives of His creation.

Therefore, those persons of wisdom who understand this concept yield to the sovereignty of God. Even the great persons of faith did not immediately acquiesce to the will of God. The *Bible* is overflowing with episodes of persons who declined to drink from the chalice of faith and perform one of the many purposes in their lives. A mature Christian comes to understand that if God tells you to do something, He expects you will. However, His plan and purpose will be accomplished regardless if any particular individual decides to be a willing participant.

When someone wants a drink immediately and a favorite cup is not available or dirty, what does he do? Naturally, he seeks a clean and available vessel. Another vessel may be conveniently located in the dish-rack, or you may have to search for one in the cupboard. But he does not fear, because there are many vessels available for his intended need. This appears to be the same manner in which God operates. There may be a reliable vessel that was initially sought. However, for some reason, it was not prepared to be used. This illustration was brought true in my life when I allowed God to use me as a willing vessel.

Last year, one Sunday afternoon after church, I decided to go to Highland Park and read a book before going to the evening service. I found an excellent location under a towering oak tree with large dark green leaves. Just as I turned off the engine, I heard an instruction in my mind's ear. It spoke the following: go to the church right now. Wait for someone who I am going to send. Was this a call from God or lack of sleep?

Now, knowing the voice of God, it was quite clear this was not a hallucination. However, I was more interested in getting what I believed was a quite well earned rest in the park. All week at work and with my friends, I had attended to the needs of others. When was it going to be my time? When would my feet get washed? I immediately placed my novel on the passenger side of the Accord and drove to the church parking lot. It was more in irritation than adoration that I yielded to the call of God's service that afternoon.

When I entered the empty parking area, I immediately looked for a prime location to park the car. This was a rare occasion that I could think about which parking spot would be strategically beneficial directly following the benediction. In hindsight, I decided that I wanted to park close to the fire. So, I decided to park next to Pastor John's slot. The parking location that displayed the pastor's name and also had another message painted in large white letters on the ground.

"Thou Shalt Not Park Here!" I believe this was the eleventh commandment Moses brought down from Mt. Sinai following his second advent.

As I sat still in the serene staging area of the church, an instance of doubt entered my mind. Possibly, I was tired and had not really heard a call to come to this place. It could have been a subconscious message from my impulsivity to always be on time. In any event, I dismissed whatever the circumstances were that drove me to my current location. I was determined to read my book and unwind for minimally one hour. This was my last opportunity for relaxation.

As I reached for my text, I noticed a woman quickly arriving on the property and heading directly for the double glass doors in the front of the church. Those feelings of doubt were now distant memories. I exited the car and walked calmly towards the woman. She was obviously distraught and determined in her demeanor.

"Can I help you?" I asked.

"I've got to get into the church. It should be open," she said in a frustrated manner.

"Services don't begin for approximately another hour," I replied. "Are you sure you are at the correct church?"

It was almost as if she didn't hear or want to hear what I told her. She frantically tried the other set of double class doors.

"I've got to get into the church. I was told that there would be a minister to meet with me," she said without directing her body towards me.

"Who were you to meet with?" I asked. "Maybe, I can be of some assistance?"

After realizing that the church was in fact locked and no one was within its hallowed premises, the woman turned and faced me. She was a young woman with almond colored skin. She was not extremely attractive. In fact, she had silent, almost mannequin like features about her. Looking deeply within her face, I could tell that at one time she had possessed more than average looks. Her thin oval face, sunken cheekbones, and deep, light brown eyes were almost hypnotic in their appearance. I gently placed my arm on her shoulder and looked directly into her eyes.

"What's wrong?" I asked.

Lowering her face into her hands, but not moving my touch from her body, she began to cry. Somewhat surprised, I moved one step backwards and returned to her the personal space she once had. It was less than a few seconds before she began to explain her situation. She was addicted to crack cocaine. Her once boyfriend and supplier was now making her prostitute herself for the illegal substance her body cried for, but certainly did not need. She further explained that the level of demand which she now required to achieve a high far exceeded her physical ability to work for the needed money.

It was at that exact moment that she stopped crying. She looked at me and placed her hands towards her sides. With no tears remaining in her eyes, she began to speak slowly.

"He told me that I wasn't making enough money on my own," she said in a barely audible voice. "He really didn't care if I was making enough money to supply my habit. He just wanted her."

"Who?" I asked.

"My baby," she replied and began to cry again.

This time, I moved closer and sat her down on the picnic benches that were just beyond the front entrance. I offered her my handkerchief from my pocket and allowed her to finish. I deliberately sat across from her and gave my undivided attention.

From the backdrop provided by the church edifice and the trees that lined the property, Cheryl shared with me that day the poor decisions that she made that led to her present state. Her boyfriend, Rick, was unconcerned that Cheryl's daughter was barely eleven. He told her that if she didn't give into to his demands, neither Cheryl nor her daughter would live to see the first snowflakes fall.

I barely noticed that cars were apparently beginning to parade down the lot. The church doors were opened, and people began to enter intermittently. I cannot recall if anyone spoke to me on his or her way into the church. It was clear that the person I was talking with was from the streets. She was scantily dressed. Her hair, although long and dark, was combed, but not styled. Eventually, the person who I was waiting for finally arrived. It was Mother Jennings. Mother Jennings did not hold any positions in the church. She was not an usher or even a member of any auxiliaries. But she had the one thing in her background that Cheryl desperately needed at the moment in her life – compassion.

As Mother Jennings walked towards the table Cheryl and I shared, I gave her an inviting look to join us.

"Mother Jennings," I said as I stood, "I would like you to meet someone special."

In her familiar inviting voice, Mother Jennings said, "Well, I would love to meet someone new today."

"Cheryl, meet Mother Jennings."

Slowly, both women moved towards each other. Before Cheryl could fully extend her hand, Mother Jennings already had her in a friendly embrace.

"Child, you come right inside, and we'll get you something to drink," she said.

It was as if Cheryl was one of Mother Jennings' own granddaughters. I saw Cheryl do something she had never done while we were together. It was something that became her very well – a smile. I later found out from Mother Jennings how Cheryl came to be at our church on that day. That very morning, she happened to be praying on the same bed used to fund her habit. After both crying and praying for some time, she said she fell asleep. While sleeping, Cheryl said she heard a voice telling her to get on the only bus that came into her inner city neighborhood and travel across town to a church to meet a pastor.

When she awoke from her sleep, she immediately walked to the edge of her neighborhood and boarded a bus. When the bus reached its final stop, she got off and walked around the neighborhood. She finally heard the church bells in the distance, which lured her to the campus. Two things about Cheryl's story hit me directly in the face.

First, of all the women in the world, God addressed and met her needs on that day. It was almost as if she was the woman of Sychar at the well – the Samaritan woman. Jesus came specifically to transform her world. Secondly, unlike me, Cheryl instantaneously obeyed the call of the Shepard. I, on the other hand, was more concerned about my own personal needs.

A sudden loud burst of laughter from one of the children immediately brought me to my present surroundings. There was no need to further delay the inevitable topic of Africa. It was a fairly long drive until we reached our home. The confined space of a minivan was not quite the best place to have an involved conversation. There was no place to escape. If the conversation became too confrontational, it would mean silent unwanted tension. At least in the home, one can move to another room or become distracted with an unpleasant task that needs to be completed.

"So, what have you decided?" Precious asked looking straight out into the distance.

I replied, "Of course we should pray first. I want to make sure that I am doing God's will. It is too easy to let self get it the way."

"I agree," Precious responded.

After quieting down the children in the vehicle, we said our family prayer.

"God is good. God is great. Lord, we thank you for this day. God bless mommy, daddy, Naomi, Christa, and Jr. God bless grandma and grandpas, aunts and uncles, nieces and nephews, cousins and friends. Bless teachers, pastors, the sick people in the hospital, and the homeless in the street. Bless everything I eat and drink. Keep us safe from danger and harm. In Jesus name we pray and for His sake. Amen."

After a brief moment of silence, I asked the Lord to guide me in my decision to go to Africa. Precious reached towards me and gently squeezed my hand. Although I was not looking in my wife's direction, I knew she was smiling. She was very excited. I cannot seem to recall the exact words I spoke that day as we drove home. In fact, it appeared that what was spoken was more of a prayer of acceptance than of guidance.

"Are you going to Africa to work with the kids Daddy?" Naomi asked.

There was silence in the car and a brief pause on my part. This was the prevailing question that was not answered, but was on the mind of everyone within the sound of its asking. Before I could form the first words from my mouth, Precious responded, "Yes honey. Daddy is going to Africa help the children."

What did I have to give? Who am I? I didn't believe that I was birthed with any special gifts. I was born in the inner city shortly after the riots following Dr. Martin Luther King Jr.'s assassination. I grew up in public housing. Whiteside Road (apartment #276) is where I began my journey in this life. The man who my mother said was my father, I only met once. It was at Jones Funeral home on Wylie Avenue in the Hill District. He was lying in an oak casket with his arms folded (motionless and emotionless). That's how I felt for much of my adolescence. I was pointlessly wandering through the streets and back alleys of my neighborhood.

There didn't seem to be anything extraordinary in my life. My first religious instruction was at a Mosque. I can remember each Saturday going to service with my sister and mother. My alcoholic stepfather never attended. I didn't see much of him on the weekends anyway. Years later, I found myself in the basement of an old Baptist church saying the sinner's prayer. My mother was a common laborer. During the week, mom sold candles downtown on Fifth Avenue.

I didn't have a stellar educational experience. I barely graduated from a public school that existed for less than ten years. In high school, I cut physical education for 3 years before I was caught in the basement (where I taught myself to play a discarded piano). I failed course after course. Mr.

Minnelli (my chemistry teacher) told me that before I was twenty-one I would be either dead or in jail. I showed him. He was only half right.

In order to serve my country (and not to evade the district magistrate), I joined the military. I was a medical specialist in the United States Army. After my honorable discharge from the Army as a sergeant, I attended California University. It was at this postsecondary institution that I obtained my bachelors of science in secondary education. Some time after teaching American literature at an inner city public school, I met and married my wife Precious Frazier. Our first children were twin girls. We later had a son, who was born in February in the same manner as his father. Obtaining my masters at the University of Pittsburgh seems like a passing vapor in my life. I remember attending some classes; however, not one friend emerged from that brief two-year stint.

All of these events were the whole of my life. I could not point to any significant experience that I had in my brief life that would equip me to work with the least, the last, and the lost on the continent of Africa. I did not recall any particular Sunday school lesson or college course that provided me with knowledge on what I may possibly face on this missionary trip. I was not aware of any particular human being who gave me insight in my life in regards to ministering to those in need.

Making this journey we call life is like a traveler at an airport. At every airport there are many destinations to take. In most of our travels, we have the ability to choose of our own will. However, there are times that the storms of life create inclement weather that makes certain choices for us. This may mean an unexpected delay or detour to reach our intended destination. In other cases, it may mean a cancellation of our plans, which may end a particular journey.

While traveling to various places in life, we often have the ability to select who set offs with us. In life, we find that there are persons placed next to us that we would have preferred not to come across. We may want to remove ourselves from their presence, but find that there are no immediate options due to the destination that we want to take at that particular moment in our lives. Our life situation dictated that those persons would be in our lives. They were divinely placed in a seat right next to us. In some cases, they may create tension, frustration, or even anger. How we endure their presence may determine or even affect our emotions.

There are many factors that determine a successful flight. Many of those elements are sometimes dynamics not associated with the vessel. There are external and internal influences that determine the elevation of a plane. Persons placed in our lives as well as individuals themselves may create turbulence and discomfort on the journey we travel. If we are wise, we learn that our attitude sometimes determines our altitude. When storms or distresses come, we quickly realize that we are not the pilots of our destination. Although we thought we were in control, there is someone else whom we cannot see that has more information than ourselves orchestrating the events in our lives. With that divine information, the proper pilot of our life knows the exact route and wants us to reach our destination at the appointed time.

We sometimes have the opportunity to select our travel companions. It would be wonderful to fill all of our journeys with persons of our choosing. Some people habitually change both partners and destinations as they travel through life. Many carelessly select persons based on the members of their bodies and not the wisdom in their minds. In countless occurrences, through patience, maturity, and divine intervention, travelers on this journey of life come across persons who bring pleasure where despair once reigned. Our journey does not seem as long and hard in their presence. Just knowing their there provides great comfort for us. We may not know exactly where their journey may end, but we are hopeful that we will be with them for most of it.

All journeys in life have multiple destinations. On my journey of life, there existed one flight plan to the continent of Africa. This itinerary had the destination of Uganda on it and the distance from my heart to the country.

It's early Saturday morning, and I am looking for sources to assist me in writing my dissertation. Now here I sit at a large wooden table at Duquesne Library. This particular level of the library was cool and silent. I found it quite tranquil on the third floor. Usually, only serious students came to that level. Athletes who needed tutoring or coeds using the facility as a singles pick-up spot generally gathered on the first or second floors.

I usually sat in the corner at a table away from the elevator and bathrooms. The unvarying ringing of the elevator bell in conjunction with the bathroom doors banging to a close were constant disturbances. These two distracters gave me strange visions of who was either coming or going. However, on this particular day, it would not have made a difference where I was at that particular moment.

I could have been on a crowded bus during rush hour or in line at an amusement park. My thoughts were consumed of the impending safari to Uganda, which was now less than six months. Of all the drama that occurred in my life during my initial meeting with Lawrence in his office, a few memories were brought to my attention that this journey would probably be more than a simple trip across the Atlantic Ocean.

These memories stemmed from the various gatherings of potential missionaries to the Ivory Coast. These gatherings came to be known simply as team meetings.

Team meetings were gatherings of those persons who were going to Uganda. It was also a manner in which to provide pertinent information to people who may have an interest in going to Africa. It was also a time for both former and current team members to tell of their experiences in Africa. The meetings were held once a month, usually on a different day of the week. These meetings would continue until a core team was formed. At these meetings, the team leader, Lawrence, would provide a forum for essential information regarding the upcoming missionary trip to Uganda.

I found these meetings to be a great asset. It was there that I learned exactly what the team would be doing when we arrived. The team was comprised of various group leaders. The group leaders had specific missions that they would pursue while abroad. There was Carol, who was currently seeking employment. She would be one of the members of the medical team. Jim, an electrical engineer, would be the group leader for the well drillers. Working in conjunction with these two team leaders were others persons who would lead groups to work with entrepreneurship, agriculture, construction, office management, security, transportation, education, and, of course, the children's ministry. I would later learn that there would be other projects to be completed while there, but these were some of the major ones.

"Welcome everyone," Lawrence said. "If you have just arrived, please sign in and fill out a name card. You may sit anywhere that you find the most comfortable."

The noise level in the room immediately went to a dull murmuring as persons found their seats. Lawrence promptly began the meeting. I sat in the rear of Wilson Hall, where the meeting was held. As my eyes scanned across the room, I looked at the many different faces, ages, and cultures. I took the time to look at every individual in that room. I wondered to myself, "What was their story? What were the various circumstances in their lives that led them to this point?"

I knew the names of some to these people from simply being a member of my church. Possibly, I spoke to them at the end of a service, or a church function that was held during some time of my tenure at Christ Church. Maybe,

I saw them briefly in the parking lot on their way to their vehicle. I knew what their voices sounded like; I may have even known their occupations. In a couple of rare cases, I was aware of the neighborhoods in which a few lived. However, in this setting, they seemed different to me some how.

At first, I thought it might have been the time at which we were gathered on the church campus. Sunday morning has a definite different feeling than Friday evening. Additionally, we were dressed more casually and relaxed. Unlike Sunday mornings when people have had a weekend to wind down and allow the previous week to slip slowly into oblivion, meeting in the evenings during the week meant that many of us brought the stress from our jobs and homes with us. Finally, there was no need to put on one's holy face. The pastor was nowhere in sight, and there was no message to be preached at that time. Additionally, there would be no offering basket to be passed around the room prior to the benediction.

None of these factors seemed to assist me in equating the distinct difference that these people had at that moment in time. Each one appeared to listen intently as Lawrence continued to provide general information about the impending trip. I finally reasoned within myself that each of these persons were on a personal mission. There had to be some reason why they purposely would leave the comforts of western civilization to camp within a third world nation. Although those persons who would be leaving with the team as married couples were in the minority, most team members would be departing the United States without their close friends, spouses, or children.

Why would a reasonable individual depart the safety and security of their home and loved ones to run plunging into a war torn nation crawling with terrorist? Looking at their faces did not provide an answer. If I knew the answer to this simple question, I would have given it to the many people within my family, workplace, and church who asked it of me. I dared not ask the others why they where going on this venture. I thought I should have known my rationale for embarking on this predestined journey. I did not want to appear ignorant of my mission and purpose. Possibly, some of the same people in the room felt exactly as I did. Were there doubts or questions in their minds about why they were going? If so, their faces definitely did not show it.

"While in Uganda, you will encounter many situations which are normal to the people there, but not to us as Americans," Lawrence said. "I am going to show you a video of a previous missionary journey taken last year to give you a sense of the region. But before I do, would everyone please stand up and give us your name. Also, tell us what team you will be on or would like to work with when we arrive in Uganda."

One by one, person by person, everyone stood up and gave somewhat of a personal testimony. As time progressed and the meetings continued throughout the year, this was typically how each one was started. Lawrence would require us to introduce ourselves, and he would provide the topic for that particular evening.

These meetings were vital to the success of the journey. For it was in these meetings that the team members began to bond with one another. We no longer gave a polite hello on Sunday mornings in passing. We actually stopped and talked with one another. We exchanged hugs, handshakes, and knowing glances as to say with our eyes, "Thanks for giving your service to others." Although a generous contributor would pay my trip in full, all the other team members had to compile about $3,500. When team members usually talked, the first question would inevitably be, "How is your fundraising coming along?" After answering, "It's going fine so many times," I felt somewhat convicted of being blessed in the matter of not having to pay my part. This was particularly difficult when I knew of various teams members who collected scrap metal or sold personal items on EBay to raise funds for the trip.

Therefore, I solicited donations from friends and family to help offset some of the cost of the trip. This included eighty-five dollars for a passport and fifty-five dollars for a visa to enter Uganda. There were many immunizations that had to be paid for along with a host of items to be packed that varied from easy on the pocket to quite costly. Once I purchased all the necessary items needed, I would secretly donate to my newly acquired friends accounts. These were tax deductible accounts set up by the church for them.

Derek, a good friend and best man at my wedding, was the first to offer to pay for my passport. A group of friends at work secretly collected money for my trip and held a surprise gathering for me shortly before my departure. Other friends mailed checks to my home or placed cash in my hands. Surprisingly, I received less than one hundred and fifty dollars from all of my family members combined. I was quite hurt by this actuality. "You can choose your friends, but not your family members." I do not know if I said this as a truth or in disappointment. However, after being forced to spend eighteen years with me and all my inadequacies, I could see why they did not particularly want to share my company. I was not by any means perfect. I had flaws in my character that needed an appendectomy.

Some people come to the realization that if it were not for the DNA that connected them to many people in this world, they probably would not have any contact with them. Our interests are different; our values and ambitions are dissimilar. This is why individuals opt for persons who are more like them in personalities that go beyond the physical and convenient.

Returning to the issue of the team meetings that occurred in the future months, it was through these gatherings that

I gained many insights regarding the region of Uganda that I was to travel to next spring. Some of the information about this region of the world that I gleaned was in regards to the climate. We were instructed on appropriate clothing that would be suitable. In one of our various meetings, we where provided with a list of items that should be packed in a personal bag for the trip.

The first item on the list was toilet paper. We were informed that any facilities were few and far in between. If the conditions of these facilities were to be improved by ten times, they could be best described as gross. Insect repellent that contained 100% deet was a must. Malaria is quite common in this section of the world. Hand-wipes to clean your hands and to refresh your face were highly recommended by members of the team who had previously attended an expedition to this particular region on Africa. Personal items such as books, periodicals, a radio, or other individual entertainment to keep you occupied during long layovers at airports were suggested.

Most importantly, any prescribed medication, hygiene products, and a secondary pair of eyeglasses were adamantly suggested. I am told that LensCrafters has yet to open a chain in the villages throughout the country. It was suggested that acquiring gently used clothing at a second hand store would be a blessing to many people. Since there are no Maytag washers or dryers to clean clothing, items worn would be left for others to use. In this way, one could not be burdened with returning with damaged or highly soiled clothing. The locals could wash donated clothing and use it for quite some time. In many cases, I am told that donated clothing is passed on to others who are in dire need.

Of all the items that appeared on the list to take to Uganda, the last item would probably be the most valuable – a camera. I was quite certain that I would return to America with souvenirs, new friendships, many stories, and images in my long-term memory. However, I needed a tangible visual representation to remind me of my experience on the continent. Precious and the children needed to see what I saw. Possibly, I needed documented evidence from for employers that I actually left the country. In any event, still or video images would probably tell the story that I could never put into words.

The final meeting prior to departure to Uganda was one that brought this trip close to home. It was a mandatory meeting for all persons who were definitely going on the trip. This meeting began as any other, except Ivan, who was in charge of security, conducted it.

"At the end of this meeting, everyone will be required to sign a waiver provided by the church council," Ivan stated as he opened his binder on the podium located in front of the room.

Lawrence said, "If you know of anyone who is going on this trip and is not present, they will have to contact me to schedule a time to sign the waiver and hear the presentation."

Lawrence seemed to have a very serious demeanor about him that day. Usually, he kept things pretty light and serene. On this particular day, there was something on his agenda that would dictate a more solemn attitude.

"The waiver that you will initial in two places and sign, releases the church from any liabilities should something occur to you while we are in Uganda. You cannot attend this trip unless you complete the forms, which will be notarized before you leave for the evening," Ivan said.

You could feel the anxious tension in the room. There was absolutely no talking occurring at the time. Even those persons who typically made short sidebar comments were attentive. Ivan was selected to be the chief of security for the team. He retired after twenty-one years as a first sergeant in the United States Marines. Surprisingly, Ivan did not go on any search and rescue mission, or at least if he did, he opted not to share that information with us. He informed us that his primary responsibilities were handling the administrative affairs of soldiers traveling abroad.

If a group of soldiers were to journey outside of the continental United States for an extended period of time, Ivan would travel with them as their administrative liaison. He would lead a team who would ensure that the deployed soldiers would continue to have such needs as salary, transportation, medical, and other supplementary needs taken care of until they returned to their base in America. This was more dangerous than it sounded like on the surface. In many instances, Ivan was deployed to regions of the world that were hostile towards the United States government and its citizens. Very few places had military bases, which meant Ivan and his team were forced to live among the local inhabitants and all of the instability that came with the environment.

"Prior to our trip to northern Uganda, I have been reading United Nations updates on the area surrounding where we will be residing during our stay. Please listen carefully to everything I am going to say to you tonight, as it may determine your level of commitment to our upcoming missionary trip."

As not to make any distraction of what would be said that evening, Lawrence left his seat and walked to the back of them room. He turned off several lights, except those in the front illuminating Ivan. This only increased my level of apprehension of what was going to be said that evening.

"U.S. citizens living in or planning to visit Uganda should be aware of threats to their safety from insurgent groups, particularly in the northern region near the border with Sudan, along the western border with the Democratic Republic of Congo, and in the southwest near the border with Rwanda. Insurgent groups have at times specifically targeted U.S. citizens. They have engaged in murder, armed attacks, kidnapping, and the placement of land mines. Although isolated, incidents occur with little or no warning," Ivan read in a very sterile voice.

He then continued to read with more intensity, "Because of continuing activity by elements of the Lord's Resistance Army (LRA) in northern Uganda, particularly the districts of Apac, Lira, Gulu, Kitgum, Pader and Adjumani, the level of violence associated with these incursions and an order to target Americans issued in May 2004 by the leader of the LRA, the Embassy strongly recommends against travel to and residence in these districts. Americans resident in these areas should review whether the LRA threats are grounds for leaving the area."

"The U.S. Embassy recommends that visitors seek up-to-date security information from park authorities before entering Mgahinga National Park and the Bwindi Impenetrable Forest National Park, both in the southwestern corner of Uganda, due to sporadic rebel activity across the Congo/Rwanda border. Rwandan rebel factions with anti-Western and anti-American ideologies are known to operate in areas of the Democratic Republic of Congo that border Uganda. One such rebel group is believed to be responsible for the March 1999 kidnapping and murder of two American and six other tourists in the Bwindi Impenetrable Forest in western Uganda, as well as the August 1998 abduction of three tourists in a Democratic Republic of Congo national park contiguous with Uganda's Mgahinga National Park," Ivan then closed his binder and opened a manila folder that was located on a shelf in the podium. He then went towards his seat.

"This is a recent article that I found from the London Times," Lawrence stated in a more relaxed voice as he turned on the lights and walked towards the podium. "Although I am not going to read the entire article to you, I will highlight some aspects of it through summarization. A copy of this article is available on the table in the rear of the room. In this particular article, Uganda's President Yoweri Museveni's government insists that the war against the LRA is being won. Recently, Mr. Museveni depicted the insurgents as a 'crushed force'. However, he has used this same depiction for over six years," Lawrence said with a smile as he continued to glance over the article.

He continued, "Recently, twenty thousand children in northern Uganda have been kidnapped by the LRA. The boys are brain washed and turned into killing machines for the rebels. Females of all ages are made sex slaves and servants for the soldiers. Many children in northern Uganda choose to flee their homes at night for fear to being captured by rebels, who burn villages and randomly kill the inhabitants. They have been called the children of the night. Over 1.7 million children have been abducted in just two years."

Kathy Coleman, the UN Security Council in New York, stated, 'Northern Uganda to me remains the biggest neglected humanitarian emergency in the world.' Hundreds of thousands of people are labeled as IDPs or internally displaced persons and live in refugee camps for fear of the LRA. Ugandan soldiers protect the refugee camps, which do not have ample supplies to feed, house, or treat medically those who hide within them," Lawrence placed the article down and looked at what would be the next team to enter Ugandan borders.

Lawrence continued, "While we are in Uganda, we will be escorted by armed police officers. They will meet us at the airport and remain throughout the duration of our missionary stay. For your safety, never go anywhere unless you inform your team leader and never go anywhere at night. We have never lost a team member and do not plan to start with this journey."

All of this seemed like too much information to process. It was all too overwhelming. If Precious had been a witness to tonight's meeting, I am quite sure her thinking of my leaving would have been greatly influenced. I'm quite sure she would have had images of our convoy being attacked or stranded. Everyone knows that it is open season on Americans around the world. We are easy targets that are high profile news stories around the world. Many terrorists view Americans as trophies to be displayed before the world as reminders of their barbaric and insidious power. There are two places that no one wants to be – a prisoner in the camp of wicked terrorists or in the hands of an angry God.

As I sat in front of my laptop computer in the library, I noticed that I had written very few words. The only thing I could see was a blinking cursor on a white page. Thinking about those meetings brought both comfort and some apprehension regarding this upcoming journey. I did not know what exactly was in store for me when I arrived in Africa. However, there was one thing that I was quite sure would not be the case this time next year. Next year, I would not be sitting wide-eyed and immature of the climate of Africa. This time next year, I would have tasted from the cistern of the Ivory Coast and have my own personal experiences on which to drawn upon. Nevertheless, for today, I would have to rely upon these reminisces of others and the trust that what they have communicated throughout these informal (but informative) gatherings would be enough to equip me for my approaching voyage.

B efore I attended my first team meeting, Lawrence informed me to contact the health department to receive the required yellow fever shot and any other recommended inoculations. I contacted the health department one evening after work by phone.

"Allegheny Health Department. How may I help you?" the voice stated on the other end of the phone connection.

"Yes. Good evening. I am traveling to Uganda in the spring. Can you tell me which shots I will need?" I asked.

"Okay. Let me just get my book out here," the woman said in a polite voice.

"Please, take your time," I replied. There was a momentary pause.

"When exactly are you planning on leaving?" she inquired.

"I have plane reservations for the third week in May," I replied.

"Alright, that is about a year. Well, the only shot that is required is yellow fever. However, there are number of other shots that we recommend that you take if you are traveling to Uganda."

"What would those be?"

"Well, we recommend that you have Hepatitis A and B, diphtheria, tetanus, measles, mumps, rubella and polio," she said patiently.

"What about typhoid and meningitis?"

"Those shots are also highly recommended, but the only shot that is required is yellow fever."

"Could you repeat those for me, I am trying to write them down?"

"Do you have a fax machine?"

"Sorry, no I don't."

"That's okay," she said in an understanding voice. "Just provide me with your home address and I will mail this information out to you. However, you need to start on many of these shots. Some have more than one series."

"Thank you very much," I added.

"By the way, you can probably get the tetanus shot from your primary care physician," she stated. "Have you had a tetanus shot in the past 5 years?"

"I can't recall," I informed her. "I will have to check with my family doctor."

"One final thing," she noted. "You will have to make an appointment for the yellow fever shot. We don't provide this vaccination everyday. It is very expensive and has to be disposed of immediately. This shot is given only on Tuesday mornings from 10:00 a.m. to 11:00 p.m. and Thursday evenings from 6:00 p.m. to 7:00 p.m. Also, you will have to stay for about twenty minutes to see if you have an allergic reaction."

"Do the prices of the immunizations vary greatly?" I asked.

"Yellow fever is probably the most expensive at $71.00," she continued. "The typhoid, which are pills you take, are $48.00 and the Meingocaccal is $64.00. The hepatitis shots are around $50.00 a piece. When I send you a list of the recommended immunizations, all these prices will be listed."

"Thank you very much."

"Also, you will need to see your family doctor to get a malaria prevention prescription," she added. "You can either take Larium or Doxy. I am sure you and your physician will decide what is best for you."

I thanked her for all the information that she provided. I made an appointment for the following day, since there was really no need to delay the inevitable. I figured that it would be best to start as early as possible. Also, it would probably be more economical to spread the cost of the immunizations over the course of a few months.

When I arrived at the health department the following day, the realization of my trip to Africa appeared to be more real. I could not find a parking space in front of the building, so I parked approximately one block away. Having worked inside all day, I thought it was good to feel the evening breeze against my face.

The entrance to the health department had somewhat of an ominous feeling. I pushed the door open with my foot and used the knuckle on my right index finger to summon the elevator. As I looked out of the glass doors that led to the busy street, I wondered what those persons looking in the window as they walked passed were thinking about persons in the health department. Of course, I had nothing to hide. However, all I needed was for a current student or coworker at my place of employment to see me. It is bad enough that rumors about me are contrived. I did not want to give them any live ammunition at this point of my career.

As soon as you walk into the building, the immediate room on the right is for the administration of HIV testing and sexually transmitted diseases. I quickly walked passed that entrance. Curiosity makes one want to look inside of that particular waiting room. However, I possessed a healthy respect for others' privacy.

Others began to gather in the area directly in front of the elevator. One had to wonder, "Why is this person here?" I did not even want to know the answer to that question. The looks on their faces were quite serious. Others' looks seemed barren and detached. The elevator finally came, and we all boarded. Luckily, one of the children who entered the elevator with an adult pushed "2", which was my exact destination to the immunization clinic.

I positioned myself strategically at the front of the elevator, as I wanted to be the first one in line when we arrived at the immunization clinic. Although I love working with young people, which was during the day, and I needed to return home and relax in order to mentally prepare for tomorrow's workday. As the door opened, I immediately exited the elevator and headed straight for the receptionist's window. I had previously been to the health clinic when I had to have a tuberculosis test read. So, I was quite aware of where I needed to report. The health department building offices were very small with signs clearly marking all areas.

When I arrived at the receptionist's window, I was greeted with a smile. This was somewhat foreign to me in that government employees are not usually friendly. I found this to be particularly true during nontraditional business hours. However, I somewhat reasoned in my mind that this clinic is more like a hospital than an office. Usually, medical personnel and those who work within medical facilities generally are personable. Even if you know they are falsifying their demeanor, you applaud their efforts.

"May I help you sir?" the woman behind the window asked.

"Yes ma'am. I am here for the yellow fever immunization," I replied. "Also, I would like to receive any other shots if I may."

Adriana, whose name I surmised from her health department identification tag, asked, "What do you need these immunizations for?"

"I am going to Uganda."

"Oh, that sounds quite interesting," Adriana answered. "When are you leaving?"

"I am scheduled to leave in May of next year," I replied.

"Well, we'll see how we can help you." Adriana replied in a friendly voice.

She provided me with a health department card that asked for both general and personal information. She instructed me to complete the card in its entirety and return to the window when I was finished. There was a cup containing pens that were available for use. However, after looking at the individuals around the room and wondering what they were here for, I decided to use my personal pen from work. Nothing against anyone personally, but I did not want to take a pen that another visitor may have needed.

I was directed to the waiting room to the right of the receptionist's window. When I entered this somewhat large room, there were people already there completing the cards and talking with one another. Some were clearly by themselves; while others were couples or families with children. Although there was really no secluded space available, I found an empty chair in front of the large picture window. I focused on the task at hand and began to diligently complete my card. The card asked for personal information such as, name, address, and telephone number. Then, there was a section inquiring the reason for your visit today and similar questions. It took less than ten minutes to neatly write the information onto the card. I carried it to the partitioned window and gave it to the receptionist.

When I finished completing the card and returned to my seat, I began to familiarize myself with my surroundings. I tried not to make eye contact with anyone else in the room while I waited for the receptionist to call my name. I began to look at the posters and maps that dressed the walls of the waiting room. There was one poster in particular that caught my attention. It was a world map that displayed where various diseases and illnesses existed. The legend listed such ailments as polio, malaria, typhoid, hepatitis and a host of others. In the United States and certain parts of Europe, the map was pretty much clear of most infectious diseases. However, the continent of Africa appeared to have every known disease known to man associated with it. This was very disheartening to view. I decided to direct my attention to other aspects while I was there. Why did I do that?

Have you ever read the information pamphlets at the health department? They are very graphic and not that encouraging. It is no wonder some people want to wear masks and live in self-contained bubbles. When your parents talked to you about communicable diseases, it was G rated. Their discussions were mostly sugarcoated with some ambiguities. On a few occasions, they may actually use words that you hear regularly on television both before and during primetime viewing. Conversely, the health department is quite straightforward. There is no time for a Mother Goose approach to education when people's lives are affected.

The images are quite graphic, but the message is clear. Every action has a reaction is the message at the health department. If you play, you will pay. Here is what it is; here are its effects. I found this approach to education to be both quite refreshing and at the same time a little disturbing. As a preacher from Clarksville, Tennessee once said, "The wages of sin is death, and you will be compensated for your actions." In this setting, there is no room for misunderstandings.

Finally, I was called to the window and directed to a room that was just opposite of the waiting room. When I entered the room, I immediately noticed the individual preparing an immunization with a syringe. Why is that?

"Is that for me?" I said somewhat jokingly.

"You guessed it," The nurse replied, as she thumped the syringe with her index finger.

I remembered as a medic in the military that this was done to remove the air bubbles from the bottom of the syringe to the top. The syringe would be recalibrated and all of the air would be pushed out of the needle.

She smiled a little; the nurse then looked at me. Her eyes directed their attention to the empty chair that was conveniently placed directly in front of her.

"Hello," she stated in a straightforward voice. "My name is Linda. I will be giving you your immunizations today. So, where are you going?"

"How do you know I'm going anywhere?" I replied. "Can't someone just take precautions and receive a yellow fever shot?" I said in a joking manner as I stared at the long shiny needle.

Linda covered her mouth and laughed. "I guess so," she said. "But in all of the many years I have been in this profession, I know that is not the case."

"I am going to Africa."

"Oh, what part?" Linda asked. "North or South Africa."

"I am going to Uganda," I stated.

"What are you going to do there?" she inquired.

"I'm a Christian missionary," I plainly said, still very aware of the needle in her hand. "I will be leading a team working with the children." I said this not only to profess my faith, but also to elicit sympathy from one who was about to pierce me with a sharp instrument.

"That sounds very interesting," she said. "This shot may be sore for a few days; so, which arm would you like to have it?"

Since I am ambidextrous, it really didn't make a difference to me. "My right arm is fine," I answered. "Will it swell or discolor?"

"I will give you a pamphlet that tells you everything you will need to know," Linda replied.

"Oh great," I thought to myself, "not another health department pamphlet. Will there be pictures in this one as well?"

"This won't hurt a bit," Linda said.

"It won't hurt you," I replied.

"Yes," she stated. "This won't hurt a bit."

With that, she administered the injection. It was quite a painless procedure, as shots go. She placed a cotton ball on my arm and instructed me to hold it.

"Now, here is the next thing we will do," Linda said.

"Is there more?" I asked.

She smiled again and handed me a box. "These are your typhoid pills," Linda stated. "There are four pills in this box. You need to take one every other day. This will immunize you for five years. Don't forget to take them as scheduled."

"Believe me; I won't," I quickly interjected.

"Now, you will have to sit in the waiting room for about fifteen minutes," she said. "You should be fine. However, if you start to feel any reaction at all, don't hesitate to ask for assistance."

I returned to the original waiting room and read the pamphlet that was provided to me. I figured it wouldn't hurt to learn as much information on the foreign substance that was now inside of my body. From the pamphlet, I learned that unlike some other immunizations, yellow fever is actually a live culture. It is prepared in embryonated eggs. I quickly learned the following four facts regarding yellow fever:

- Yellow fever is a tropical disease that is spread to humans by infected mosquitoes.
- Many yellow fever infections are mild, but the disease can cause severe, life-threatening illnesses.

- Yellow fever is found only in Africa and South America.
- Yellow fever is preventable by immunization. Travelers to countries with yellow fever should get the yellow fever vaccine.

After reading the entire pamphlet, I noticed that the time limit for waiting had passed. I stopped passed the receptionist's window and said good-bye to Adriana. I was careful not to read or look at any of the posters that were displayed by the elevator as I waited. I rode the elevator alone down to the first floor. This was an event that clearly indicated my commitment to the missionary journey. I felt a new surge of energy at that very moment.

As I was heading out of the health department building, I was pushing the door to the outside and a woman was pushing it towards the inside. It was Cheryl and her daughter. I immediately thought the worse as I looked at her daughter.

"Hello Cheryl," I said. "How are you doing?" This seemed to be a brainless question to ask someone going into the health department. But this is what happens when people speak without really thinking first. It had been quite some time since we last talked. Although she did not attend our church, I did learn that Mother Jennings connected her with a ministry that helps recovering addicts. It was located not too far from where Cheryl lived. Cheryl looked remarkably different than the initial time we had met. Her face did not seem as dark and ominous. Her lips were not dry and cracked. Her skin looked much healthier than before. Cheryl's cheeks were not sunken as they once were.

"Not that good," she said. "I had to take an AIDS test in the program I am in. I got a call and found out that I tested positive. I come here for my treatments twice a week."

Without any regard for my well-being or of contracting anything, I gave her a hug and told her I was sorry. As I hugged her, she placed her head on my shoulder and whimpered a little, but did not cry.

"I knew it would happen," she said as she held back her tears.

I had no words for her at that moment. All I could do was look into her eyes, so she could see my concern. I knew she had a host of questions within herself. I knew she was concerned about her daughter. She informed me that her former boyfriend was arrested, and she no longer lived in her previous apartment. Cheryl was living in a woman's shelter that had three room efficiency apartments. Her daughter was back in school, after missing almost an entire year. All the news was not bad. She still kept in contact with Mother Jennings and a few other ladies at our church.

"What's your name beautiful?" I asked her daughter.

"Morgan," she said shyly hiding her face behind her mother's arm.

"That's a pretty name," I replied.

"Ma'am," a woman who appeared to work at the health department said. "We are about to close shortly. Do you have an appointment?"

"Yes, I do," Cheryl replied.

"Do you need a ride home?" I asked.

"No," she stated. "The van driver from my building dropped me off. He's in the parking lot waiting."

"Well, I will let you go," I said. "I'm praying for you, and I am hopeful that everything works out for you and Morgan."

"God is in control," she said as she entered the building.

I was somewhat relieved that Cheryl and her daughter had a ride. I don't think I could have survived a ride with her for any length of time and enduring the many hardship stories she would tell. I knew my wife had been praying for her for quite some time since I told Precious about Cheryl. I called my wife on my cell phone and gave her an update on

Cheryl's situation. I love my wife. She has such compassion and genuine concern for people. I could hear it in her voice as I relayed the entire episode as best I could without getting emotional.

I didn't need that particular drive home alone that evening. I talked with Precious as long as I could before she had to hang up the phone in order to put the twins and Jr. to bed. After all, it was a school night. As I contemplated Cheryl's predicament, I thought about the millions of Africans and people around the world who have AIDS and no medical assistance.

In one of our meetings, I remember Lawrence telling us what a United Nations warning stated about AIDS in the area of Uganda where we were to be stationed.

I recalled him saying, "The prevalence of communicable diseases and infectious diseases is so high, that you will have to assume that everyone that you come into contact with has either AIDS or some form of hepatitis." Those words will be with me a very long time.

I turned the radio off as I pressed the garage door opener and entered our silent home. Everyone was asleep. I went to the twins' room and gave each of them a kiss and covered them with their Veggie Tales bedding. I went to Jr.'s room and noticed him sleeping on top of his favorite blanket. I did not disturb him, but I did provide him with a kiss as well. I showered, brushed, and went to bed; by this time, Precious was desperately asleep. As I lay there silently thinking about what could be possibly going through Cheryl's head that night, Precious, while yet soundly asleep, cuddled next to me and put her arm around me. I am hopeful Cheryl's daughter feels that same love as I do right now.

When I walked into my office the next morning, I was immediately confronted with a question by a coworker. His name was Richard Skye. He liked to be called Skye. For some reason, he enjoyed posing both philosophical and practical questions to me. Initially, they were quite sporadic at the beginning of our tenure together at the college; however, recently, they became more consistent as our relationship as officemates progressed. Although he never admitted it, he was a born again atheist. At one time he was a member of a place of worship. However, as he put it, "I put my brain back in my head and walked out the church."

Initially, I did not know how to take our interactions. There were instances when Skye was attentive to what I had to say and seemed very engaging. On other occasions, his curt attitude and sarcasms could cut directly to the noblest man's heart. Skye's manic attributes and behaviors were probably enough to drive a holy man to the state store. Depending on how I felt on a given day, I would self prescribe my interactions with him. I did not mind being a light in darkness and the salt of the earth. However, even Jesus took time off from his family, friends, and enemies.

"So what's your question Skye?" I asked in a polite voice.

"When was the most segregated time in American history?" Skye asked.

This seemed to be a straightforward question. However, when you are an instructor at a junior college, and an instructor of liberal studies poses this question to you, something is up.

"Well, don't just stand there waiting for NASA to name the next planet, answer my question."

"Give me a minute," I said.

Two possible answers came to me. Initially, I thought the period during American slavery. I was cautious not to be tricked in a civil war of words with Skye to decide if the Confederate states were a part of America. So, I saw a little of his entrapment there. However, if I did not point out the era in America from 1619-1865, possibly he would point out the enslavement of a race of people. Still, this seemed too obvious of an answer.

"Come on Joshua," Skye said probably in the same way the serpent told Eve to make applesauce. "Answer the question. You're a smart guy."

Luckily, the phone on his desk rang. It appeared from the first few seconds on the phone, someone called that he definitely wanted to converse with for some time. This gave me time to think more about his question. Of course, I fully understood that whatever my response would be, it would be assaulted inevitably with callous condemnation. No one can really predict the intentions of other persons at all times. However, in this case, I knew something was rotten in the state of Pennsylvania.

The second possible answer was during the 1950's and 1960's. However, obvious was not always accurate. But I reasoned within myself. How could anyone overlook Jim Crow laws? What about the landmark case of Brown v. The Board of Education? No one in his or her right mind believed separate but equal was anything but incommensurable. No one but Richard Skye could do so. However, it was close to lunch, and I just left a freshman American literature class, and I was exhausted.

"Thanks for calling," Skye said as he hung up the phone. He then directed his attention to me.

"So, I guess you want my answer," I said.

"Do I need to repeat the question?"

"No. I believe I have my answer," I replied. "However, I already know you have something up your sleeve."

"Just answer the question!" he said excitedly.

"I would have to say the most segregated time in American history would have to have been during the 1950's and 1960's," I responded. "Given both the political and cultural climate, this appears to a very intense time in American history."

"I am sorry; you're wrong."

My first impression was to question him. However, I yielded and gave my second response. I guessed that it would probably be the only other justifiable response.

"Would you care to try again friend?" Skye asked.

"I will have to say that American slavery between 1619 through 1865."

"Oh, I'm sorry. You're wrong again. Thank you for your time."

"What do you mean?" I said. "What other possible, reasonable answer could there be? Are you referring to the period before the woman's suffrage moment?"

"Alright my friend. Since I like you and you seem to be getting a little frustrated, I am going to provide you with the answer."

"That would be nice. I'm anxious to hear to your answer."

"The most segregated time in American history is every Sunday morning," he said with a smile and turned towards his bookshelf.

For a mere instant, I was somewhat bewildered. However, the essence of his response was not lost on me. I could or would not challenge his philosophy; however illogical or ominous it may have appeared on the surface. He did not turn around from his chair as I stood there facing him. However, I could still see in my mind his smiling wide-eyed face.

When I thought about his answer and worked it over in my mind. In some regards, it was true. Monday through Saturday, Christians attend school together, live next door to one another, spend many hours at work together, but separate for a few hours on Sunday morning. In many cases, this separation is by the cultural dynamics of the congregation. Also, there is a separation of Christians by socioeconomic status. The well to do Christians generally are miles away from those Christians who come from a low economic background.

There were many other separation dynamics that crossed my mind, as I stood there silent. I tried to reason from within myself why this was so. If Jesus is the central figure of the Christian church, then why is there such disunity among his followers? Twelve people started a movement that created one church. Currently, there are over 6,000 different denominations of Christianity around the world.

The further history is removed from the date of the crucifixion, the more denominational births occur. The latest trend is ten percent of Americans attend some form of home church group. Societal trends have informed us that when fifteen percent of the population engages in a certain behavior, it becomes a permanent part of the culture. What will be the end result? Will the Christian church as it now exists come to an end? At some point, will the doors of the traditional church be locked and every family household will have its own church? The mere thought of it was unfathomable.

"I have to run to my next class," Skye said. "You have a good evening." He exited the office as I finally sat down in my chair. While I was sitting there, I logged into my e-mail. I came across a letter from Emmanuel. Emmanuel was from Rwanda. He came to the United States as a seminary student from Uganda. The first time that we met was one Sunday afternoon after church. I can recall our first meeting that day and when he came to our home for dinner.

"Now may the grace of our Lord Jesus Christ be with you all both now and forever," the pastor said as he extended his arms outward towards the sanctuary.

"Amen," the congregation responded.

As my wife and I exited from the pews, I proposed in my heart to meet Emmanuel. He was introduced to the congregation earlier this year. We were informed that he would be at Trinity Seminary for one year to complete his masters in divinity. The congregation had been informed that he was an exchange student from a college somewhere in Uganda.

"Joshua," Precious said. "I am going downstairs to children's church to collect the girls and Jr."

"That's good," I responded. "I am going to introduce myself to Emmanuel."

"How nice. I'll see you," she said. Precious gave me a kiss and walked towards the rear of the church.

I always wanted to meet Emmanuel, but my hectic schedule of family life, postgraduate school, and instructing at the college occupied a major portion of my life. However, since I decided to travel abroad, my senses were heightened on any aspect dealing with not only Uganda, but Africa as well. I hurriedly walked over to the pew Emmanuel was standing near. He was talking with C. J. Brooks, a member of the church who was also a student at Trinity Seminary.

"Good morning gentlemen," I said with a smile as I extended my hand to Emmanuel.

"Good morning sir," Emmanuel said with a secure, but gentle handshake.

"Hey, Joshua," C. J. said as he placed his arm around my shoulder. "How are things going?"

"Very hectic, as you can imagine C. J.," I responded.

"That's the way it is when you are in school," C. J. said. "How is your doctoral work coming along? I don't know if I will be ready to take that next step."

"Everything in God's time," I said. Turning to Emmanuel, "Hello my name is Joshua Hopkins."

"It is a pleasure to meet you sir," he said. I am called Emmanuel Nyakoojo. I have heard you read the scriptures in the past. You do quite well."

"Thank you very much. It's very intimidating to speak in front of such a large congregation."

"Yes, I suppose it can be up there on the pulpit," he said.

"Emmanuel, I would love to have you as a guest in our home soon."

"I would love too," Emmanuel said.

"What about me?" C. J. asked.

"We had you in our home many times before C. J. I didn't think you were up to another visit so soon," I said jokingly.

"Thanks for the offer Joshua," C. J. said. "I'm sure Emmanuel will enjoy himself with your family."

"Well," I said, "how about it Emmanuel? Do you still care to come to our home?"

"Yes, please," he replied as he pulled out a small thin notebook. "Let me give you my number at my apartment. Do you have an Internet address?"

"Well, yes I do. Actually, it would probably be more convenient to contact me by e-mail. I believe I have a business card in my wallet."

We exchanged numbers and e-mail addresses as we walked out of the sanctuary. I was excited at the opportunity to spend time with someone from Africa. We acknowledged others as we continued on our way out.

"I look forward to hearing from you soon," he said.

"I will send you an e-mail this week," I replied. "Have a good evening."

"You as well." He reconnected with C. J., and they walked outside towards the Barn Café with a group of seminary students.

"Daddy!" a voice yelled behind me. It was Jr. with what appeared to be a colored paper plate in his hand.

"What is this?" I asked gesturing toward his art project.

"I made it in class," he answered.

"Hey honey," Precious said walking towards me with the girls trailing closely behind her in their matching sundresses. "Did you get to speak with Emmanuel?"

"Yes I did," I replied as I gave her a little kiss on her cheek. "I will probably contact him sometime later this week."

In fact, it was he who had contacted me. I received the first of many e-mails that he and I would send across the World Wide Web both inside and outside of the continental United States. I selected the letter with the subject "Meeting" that came from him and read the contents:

To: Joshuaone9@Christplanet.net
From: minemmanuel@Christplanet.net
Subject: Meeting

Hello Joshua. I was very glad to meet you on Sunday. The people at the church have been extremely kind to me during my brief stay here in America. I have met many new friends and am very grateful. I have reviewed my schedule for the next few weekends. I have to prepare for a test this weekend. I am available the following two weekends after twelve noon. Have a good day and God bless you very much.

I quickly replied with enthusiasm to Emmanuel's letter:

To: minemmanuel@Christplanet.net
From: Joshuaone9@Christplanet.net
Subject: Meeting

Hello Emmanuel. I am hopeful that this e-mail finds you well. Thank you for responding to me so quickly. I, as well, was excited to meet you on Sunday after church. Saturday, the fourteenth at twelve o'clock is fine. I can come to the campus to pick you up for a visit in our home. The school is about one hour from our home. I assume that you live in the apartment building behind the seminary. Please provide me with your apartment number. If this time is not acceptable, please inform me of a better time. Have a great day and outstanding week.

After two days, I received the following reply from Emmanuel:

To: Joshuaone9@Christplanet.net
From: minemmanuel@Christplanet.net
Subject: Saturday the 14th

Hello Joshua. Twelve noon sounds very good. I look forward to seeing you then. God be with you my friend.

Late that Saturday morning, I eagerly waited for the time that I would spend personally with Emmanuel. I invited a few friends over to my house as well to meet him. I told a couple of my friends, "When is the next time that you will meet someone from Rwanda?" They agreed that this would be a great opportunity and would meet me at my home for an early dinner. As I drove down to the seminary, I wondered how the day would go. Is there some custom that I was not aware of that would insult him? Would he enjoy our food? I said a brief prayer and continued down Ohio River Boulevard. I decided to continue with what has worked for me all my life – just be who I am.

As I pulled up to the apartment building, I could see Emmanuel waiting just behind the double glass doors. He stood there still with a small black bag in his hand. I parked directly in front of the door and gestured with my hands for him to come to the car. He was already looking in my direction as I was parking. He walked towards the car. His bright smile was a refreshing welcome to what had been somewhat of a rainy morning.

"Hello Emmanuel," I said.

"Good morning Joshua," he responded. "Did you find your travels here okay?"

"Yes. I didn't have much trouble finding the school. This is the first time that I have been on the campus."

"That's good."

"So, are you ready to go?"

"Yes, please."

As we drove away from the campus, I thought to myself that I did not want to overwhelm Emmanuel with too many questions. However, I felt compelled to probe into his experiences to assist me in my understanding of a continent that I had never touched. As I told my friends, "When is the next time that you will have the opportunity to speak with someone from Africa?" I began to ask Emmanuel some general question about his time at the seminary. He appeared to provide me with basic responses. However, there were two personal questions that I asked him that I found quite interesting as I began to understand his perspective as a foreign visitor.

"So, Emmanuel," I said, "how did you get selected to come to America?"

"I believe that it was my destiny to come here," he replied. "I was born in Rwanda in a placed called Ruhengeri. It is north of Kagali, the capital city. I worked as a Sunday school teacher in my church for many years. Later, I was asked to be the full time youth pastor."

"How much did that job pay?" I asked.

He smiled a little and replied, "Most of the churches in Rwanda have no money to pay people. I did this job without financial support."

"How did you live and survive?"

"In Africa, the people take care of the workers of God. I stayed with my extended family members. They are shop-keepers who trade merchandise for various goods they need."

"That sounds very honorable."

"Thank you. Well, after some time, a leading pastor of the diocese heard of the good work that I was doing at my church. So, out of 27 churches, he selected me to attend UCU."

"What is UCU?"

"Sorry, please forgive me. UCU are the initials for Uganda Christian University. The school is so well known in my area that I forget many people here in America have not heard of it. But, it is a very famous college that people from hundreds of miles in several countries in Africa travel to for an education. People from Uganda, Kenya, Rwanda, Tanzania, the Congo and other areas attend that school."

"Tell me more."

"Well, let me first tell you a few things about its location. UCU is about 23 kilometers from the capital city of Kampala on the main road to Jinga. It actually located in a place called Mukono. It was started about ninety-five years ago in order to train church leaders. It has about 3000 students."

He then handed me a card with the following words printed on the top: Rules of Life.

"Read this. This will give you a better perception of the University."

"How do all these different people get along and communicate with one another? It sounds like it would be very difficult to communicate with one another with all these different languages."

He smiled again and said, "This is a common question that I have been getting here in America. Many people do not understand that although there are thousands of languages on the continent of Africa, the one unifying tongue is English."

"So, English is spoken on campus?"

"Correct. Many of the professors are from other the countries that the students come from and can speak their native tongue. However, English is the language of instruction. This environment is good for the people because at meals and in the dorms we try to learn one another's tongue."

As Emmanuel was speaking about how the various people in Africa sought to understand each other, two things immediately came to mind. One was from a scene on the slave ship in the film *Roots*. One slave spoke in English to the other captives to learn the language of their brothers from Africa who were from various areas in order that they may unite. When Emmanuel so clearly explained to me they eagerly sought to learn about one another's differences, it occurred to me that I was less advanced than I perceived them to be.

The students at UCU were postsecondary learners who spoke in two to three languages minimally from childhood. I only spoke standard American English at work and slang when playing basketball back in my "hood". Although I do not believe "ghetto" is an officially recognized official language. In many areas around the world, people are forced to learn more than one language as they travel from country to country or town to town in their regions. This holds true for Europe, Asia, and apparently Africa. Living in cities from

California to New York and traveling from the Midwest to the panhandle of Florida, I had taken for granted that the entire region speaks English. I had no need to learn other cultural norms or languages when I traveled throughout the United States. Even when I traveled to Niagara Falls and the Bahamas, I felt quite at home using my American tongue and customs. It was only in talking with Emmanuel that I realized that being aware of other customs and languages around the world is vital to your survival.

As we rapidly approach my home, Emmanuel shared many things about his experiences in America. I learned many things about American culture through his eyes. Some aspects were so automatic that I had not thought of them as being so divergent from other cultures in the world.

"What is the one thing that you have noticed about Americans?" I asked.

"Please do not be offended at my response."

"Oh no, I won't," I replied. "I want a true and honest perspective."

"Alright; it appears that many Americans have a great concern for time."

"Could you please explain further?"

"It is almost as if they have little time for many things."

"Could you give me an example?"

"In Africa, we eat all our meals together sitting down. In America, people eat in separate rooms or even while driving in their cars. Also, after church or while meeting on the street, they are always in a rush. This must make it difficult to build strong relationships. In our village, we have a custom. Every morning, everyone checks on all their neighbors around him or her to see if they have made it through the night. This is done even before wood or coal is gathered to make breakfast."

"The spread of AIDS and other diseases has made this custom even more needed. Also, the threat of predators is a major problem. We have a black snake whose bite kills within seconds. Malaria is common among most of the people who cannot afford a mosquito net to protect them. There is even a rat that breathes on your skin first before it eats your flesh to numb it, and you won't know you have been bitten until the next morning. We all need someone else for his or her survival. You have those who plant, herd cattle, gather coal or water, build shelters, and other things."

I thought to myself as he was talking that everyone cannot do everything, but everyone can do something. This is how relationships help the entire community. It is quite possible that the modern conveniences in Western culture may have eliminated the need of dependence on others in many areas.

I had no response as we pulled into the back of my driveway. However, I made no motion to exit the car. There was still a question I had for Emmanuel before our private time would end probably for the remainder of our lives. I wanted to know his perspective on this multicultural environment that he had been thrust into in America.

"How have you been treated by others from diverse cultures here in America?"

"The people at the seminary and church treat me quite well."

"I am quite sure of that. But I am talking about once you leave those environments. Have you been to our malls or downtown areas? How do total strangers in businesses and on the street treat you?"

"One thing that I have noticed is that I am being sheltered from total American society in many ways. I get the feeling that if I were left on my own, I would not receive equal service from many strangers as I have had when I am with my American friends. I sense that there is something in American dealing with people of color that is concealed from me. However, I can assume that it is somewhat similar to tribal differences, only it is based on color and economical differences."

I decided that I had no right to give my narrow opinion of one American. I opened the car door and entered our home. My wife and children greeted us in the family room. After giving me a little kiss, my wife gave Emmanuel a hug, as all my children did as well. Like me, my children had many questions for him. I could see that their concept of Africa was similar to mine, only on an elementary level.

"Do people in Africa have clothes?" Christa asked.

Emmanuel smiled and stood. "What am I wearing young one?" he said.

"Oh," she responded and laughed as she hid behind my chair.

Those and many other questions from my family barraged Emmanuel. I did not grow tired of hearing his explanations. The doorbell sounded, and I excused myself from the room. It was Ron and his wife Stacey. I welcomed them into our home and introduced the couple. Initially, Ron asked him questions about the government in Rwanda. Stacey's questions were concerning the churches in the country. It seemed that most of his interactions with Americans were probably the same as they were tonight. However, he seemed to enjoy our fellowship together.

Knowing that Emmanuel was from Rwanda, there were many questions that we had about the tribal wars. Although he prefixed his discussion about how many people did not want to talk about the situation between the Tutsis and Hutus, he said he would share one experience from Rwanda.

"That evening started as hundreds before had. My family was sitting down to have our evening meal in our village. Suddenly, we heard screams from outside. I ran to the window and saw one of the young girls from our village totally naked and bleeding. She yelled, "'Hutus! Hutus!'"

"What our village feared most was finally happening. Since most of the people in my village were respected shop owners, we thought we would be spared from the massacres. But, this was not to be. Screams exploded from the houses of my friends. Women were carrying children and running into the bush. I could see some men coming down our road carrying machetes. They burst in some of the homes that lined the roads. Their machetes were dripping of the blood of my neighbors."

"We had planned for this event. Many of the homes in our village were connected together. We had passages that went from house to house. The last home had a secret exit that led to a path directly deep into the bush. My mother sent my sisters to the passage to our neighbor's house. My two younger brothers were at the well at the other end of the village collecting the evening water. I went towards the door that my mother had clearly blocked with her body."

"She would not let me out."

"I begged her, but she would not relent. In a voice that I had never heard my mother use, she ordered me to secure my sisters. Without thinking, I ran through the homes and found myself on the path heading through the tall grass. As I ran through the brush, I heard a child crying. It was Phillip, an orphan who was cared for in our village. I picked him up and carried him with me. I heard screams coming from our village as I ran in the distance. When I looked back, I could see the large black clouds of smoke just beyond where we were standing."

"My sisters almost knocked me to the ground when they embraced me in tears. When they did not see our mother or brothers, they began to cry all the more. We looked for more people to come from our village. I told everyone to be quiet and sit down. We did not want to be discovered out there defenseless. Whatever would happen next, we knew we would be spending the night out there. It was common for the raiders to take possessions and valuables. Sometimes, they would make several trips to steal the belongings of others."

"I don't think anyone slept that night. There were continuous streams of muffled cries. When there was just enough sun to light our path back to the village, we moved slowly and cautiously through the bush."

Without warning, Naomi asked, "What happened next?"

It was as though he realized that he was not only telling his story, but also reliving it – right in front of our eyes. He looked around the room at us and then he looked into Naomi's eyes.

"Well," he said, "I found my mother and youngest brother. She told me that they were in the house of the village elder. When the Hutus came in, they walked right past them. It was if they were invisible. The men took a few things and left the home."

"When we came to our home, we looked at the damage the men caused. I heard my sister yell. We ran toward the sounds of her cries. In my mother's room in the closet was Joseph. He was barely breathing, but alive. He had been stabbed several times. Mother went to him and hugged him. The blood from his chest was all over her face and dress. She squeezed Joseph close to her. He called her name. She placed her ear next to his mouth. He whispered something into her ear. He coughed a few times and became very still and died in my mother's arms."

I can't seem to remember exactly what else happened that night. However, I do know we all made a new friend that today. As I was emptying my pockets into the top drawer of my dresser, I came across the card Emmanuel gave to me that evening. It contained what appeared to be 10 beliefs of the institution. As I read them, I immediately noticed a cultural difference between this African Anglican institution and the

American Christian churches. Their positions are clear and direct. The card read as follows:

Seeking to love our neighbours as ourselves.

1. We shall worship the one true God and avoid polytheistic worship and the invoking of ancestral spirits or other powers.
2. We shall avoid swearing and disparaging talk about God, or gossip about our neighbour.
3. We shall respect public times of worship and rest.
4. We shall respect the legitimate authority of the state, the family, the Church and the University. We shall observe University rules and not participate in any public riot. Conviction of criminal, civil, or professional offences will be grounds for discipline by the University.
5. We uphold the human and civil rights of persons regardless of race, class, ethnic group, or gender, including the unborn, and we renounce any physical or verbal abuse of another person.
6. We shall shun all sexual immorality, polygamy, adultery, fornication and homosexual practice.
7. We shall not steal or engage in financial dishonesty of any kind.
8. We shall tell the truth and renounce all forms of plagiarism and false testimony.
9. Men and women will dress decently and will treat each other with decency and purity.
10. We shall exercise moderation in all things, avoiding the abuse of body and soul by tobacco, drugs, pornography, or gambling. Use of alcohol is prohibited on campus, and drunkenness is an offence against the community.

As I completed my reading of this card, I wondered how the American or world Christian church would be if they subscribed to all of these rules of life. In thinking about some of these rules of life, many countries around the world are diametrically opposed to many of them. Even the business community or common man would find it very difficult to adhere to all of these rules. Yet, people from simple and modest backgrounds are charged to do this on a continual basis. In America, I read bumper stickers about tolerance. I see programs on television about respecting others opinions. I wonder if tolerance and respecting others opinions would apply to UCU's rules of faith. It would appear that many believe in our "advanced and civilized" culture that intolerance must apply to those things we don't tolerate.

I reviewed my school's mission statement. It was quite general and politically correct. It dealt primarily with academic achievement. All the correct verbiage was present in it. It was quite monotonous and sterile in its implication. No one would be offended or enlightened by its meaning.

The Ten Commandments seemed easier to adhere to than some of these rules set forth by UCU. Many of the rules were things that are commonplace in my culture. They are practices that are done without precaution or remorse. They are encouraged and celebrated in the media and practiced in everyday life. I cannot honestly say that I am in adherence to all these rules of life. If this is the culture I am going to face in Uganda, then I have much to come to terms with in my own life. What appeared to be a simple missionary journey has grown into a personal confrontation of cultures and ideals.

The house seemed a little different today. I was alone in the game room prepared to take one final inspection of my luggage. Many feelings came over me, as I stood alone in that room. There was a feeling of excitement. In less than 24 hours, I will be in the beauty of the Netherlands and then onto the plains Africa. I also felt some sadness. In less than 24 hours, I will be flying over a vast ocean thousands of miles and continents away from those whom I love. Finally, I felt the peace of the Lord. In less than 24 hours, I would be a modern day Apostle Paul taking the gospel to the least, the last, and the lost.

I completed packing all three of my bags. We were permitted to take four bags. Lawrence packed one bag for each member of the team to travel with to Uganda. He called it a team bag. In this bag, Lawrence placed items specifically needed for the various ministries. I weighed the team bag on my bathroom scale. It weighed 48 pounds. The Airline permitted check-in baggage to weigh no more than 50 pounds. Any bags weighing over 50 pounds would have a $25.00 charge attached. The second largest check-in bag contained all clothing for others and myself. Since I was only staying for a about two weeks, I carefully decided what I thought was essential. My bag weighed 50 pounds. Precious and I decided that we could place some of the children's clothes in the luggage to distribute.

So, I placed children's clothes and a few pair of children's shoes in my luggage to take with me to Uganda. There remained room for three business dresses that Precious wanted to donate. One of the two pieces of luggage that I was carrying on the aircraft with me was a laptop computer. Although many people read and listen to music while waiting in the airport, I figured that I would work on my dissertation. In addition, I also knew that I could spend an ample amount of time reviewing my presentations for the conference in Uganda. I was scheduled to provide five presentations for a one-day conference for people who wanted to start neighborhood clubs in their communities.

After corresponding with Sarah, my Ugandan contact, for over 10 months, it was decided that the best way to minister to the children in Uganda was to start children's clubs. It was decided that they would be called ENK-U clubs. ENK-U was an acronym for every neighborhood kid Uganda. We thought that the best way to help the children was to have responsible adults in every area throughout the region conduct weekly club meetings on Saturday mornings or Sunday afternoons for about one hour. During that time, the club leaders could assess the children's concerns as well as their families.

Additionally, the club members could use this time to help those in the community who were in need of some assistance. The club meetings would consist of singing, prayer, biblical instruction, and fellowship. Whenever possible, we would also provide some sort of nourishment for the children.

Many of the children who were in the ENK-U clubs were refugees displaced due to political unrest in the area. The stories that Sarah sent to me regarding the hardships that these children faced were beyond heart wrenching. The death, disease, and displacement of these youth not only made me have compassion, but anger. I suddenly felt anger against those who were inflicting this type of undue pain on innocent children. I wanted to help; I knew I had to help.

The ENK-U clubs were nice and a great way to build a relationship with the children. However, it was not enough to mend the lifelong damage caused by rebel forces in the area and the lack of government intervention. There had to be something more I could do. Nonetheless, was I willing to pray the ultimate price?

The second piece of carry-on luggage contained a couple of pairs of clothing. This was done just in case my bags did not make it to their final destination. I also had my malaria medication and other toiletries that were essential for this trip. Naturally, I had many sweets and salty snacks I would snack on while in Africa. I do not believe that there is a Wal-Mart in the villages I can go to when I wanted a Butterfinger in the middle of the night.

"What have you been doing all this time while I drove the children to school?" Precious asked.

We decided that it was best for me to say good-bye to the children before they left for school that morning. Since only passengers were permitted beyond the security area to reach their gates, it would not be beneficial for the children merely to take me to the front doors of the airport and drive away. We decided a hearty good-bye breakfast would be more meaningful and memorable.

"I was just thinking dear," I replied.

"You have been doing a lot of that over this last year."

"I believe something extraordinary is going to take place on this trip."

"I believe so too honey," Precious continued. "You are one of the greatest teacher's in the world," she replied.

Precious came close to me and gave me an affectionate embrace.

"You know I'm going to miss you."

"I miss you already Precious," I said with my eyes closed tightly as my arms were around her.

At that particular moment in time, nothing seemed to exist outside of our embrace. The silence of the room was only broken by the sounds of our gentle breathing. I moved Precious slightly away from me and looked into her bright brown eyes. Unexpectedly, she gave me one of the most passionate kisses we have had since our marriage. Our lips were as one and our entire bodies followed very soon after. It's amazing what you can do in 23 minutes when you really put your mind to it. Precious was very thorough.

All the way to the airport, Precious held my hand in the car. Gospel music was playing softly in the background. Every so often, I would look over at Precious to admire her beauty. I pretended that I was looking in the passenger side view mirror. Somehow, I think she knew what I was actually doing. Even after eight years of marriage, I still was nervous around her during our intimate moments. I don't believe that I will ever get used to her.

It didn't really matter. I knew that we would have a long and loving marriage. She supported me in just about every divine and harebrained idea. I was lucky to have Precious as my wife. I was more blessed to have Precious as my best friend.

"I will go to the departure side of the airport," I said. "I'll check my bags with the porter and meet the team at the airline check-in gate on the inside."

I maneuvered around the jersey barriers and parked the car in front of my airline carrier's departure desk. I exited the car and motioned towards one of the porters.

"I'm going to miss you so much Joshua," Precious said.

Precious gave me a kiss and hugged me around my neck. The porter smiled as he took the luggage out of the trunk. We finally separated, and I walked towards the entrance of the airport terminal.

"Call me as often as you can."

"You know I will Precious," I said as I waved excitedly. I had a surprise for her when she returned home. On our kitchen table, I placed a CD of my voice. The CD is a daily 10-minute *Bible* study recording. I made it at work. It begins with me reciting the disciples' prayer that Jesus taught his followers. Next, I invite the listeners to join me in our family prayer. It also contains a daily reading of different chapters in the *Bible*. Following the reading, a brief lesson is presented. I read dramatically to keep the attention of my children. I give a brief explanation of the text. I made one for every day that I would be away from home.

I also placed a huge gift basket at the foot of the bed. The basket is covered in plastic. At the very top is a large yellow bow that is made from a wide ribbon. Contained in this basket are perfumes and colognes. Two hand towels and bath towels are rolled neatly at the back of the basket. Scented colored candles line the perimeter of the basket. There are two inspirational books for each gender. Also, there are soaps and lotions. Finally, there is a bottle of champagne and two crystal glasses. I am hopeful that we may enjoy this small token of my love upon my return.

When I arrived in the area of my airline, I noticed various members of the team. They were congregated near the arrival and departure signs.

"Joshua," someone called. "Over here."

I turned in the direction of the voice. It was Carol. She will be charge of the medical team and health education. Carol finally obtained a position as registered nurse at an assisted living complex.

"Hey Carol," I responded with a beam.

"Are you ready to go honey?"

Carol was from Dripping Springs, Texas. She was a tall fair-haired woman with the cliché southern hospitality personality. Carol hugged everyone she met in an amorous manner. She looked at you square in the eye with her bright infectious smile.

"I guess I'm as ready as I'll ever be."

"That's the spirit," Carol replied. "Let's join the other team members."

As we walked toward the other members, Devonte' and the pastor were herding the group towards a corner in a secluded area. Devonte' will be in charge of the team until we arrive in Uganda. Lawrence and seven other members left a week ago. They were the advance team that would prepare everything for our arrival in Africa. Devonte' had been on every previous mission trip since the church started this ministry. Devonte' motioned his arms for everyone to make a circle. Pastor John began to speak.

"I see Joshua and Carol have arrived safely," he said. "Let's ask God to bless you as you embark on this great missionary journey."

"Remember what Jesus said when you pray Pastor," Devonte said.

"And what might that be?" asked Pastor John.

"What thou doest, do it quickly," Devonte'said. "We have a plane to catch."

Various members of the group laughed. We all knew Pastor John loved to speak, especially when he had a captive audience.

"As Henry VIII said to each of his six wives, I'm not going to keep you long."

We all joined him in a laugh, which broke the tension that each of us were feeling.

"Dear Lord, I asked that you bless every member on this team and their families as they go to Uganda to do your work. Help them to overcome unforeseen circumstances. Keep them safe from hurt, harm, and danger that is seen and unseen. Allow their entire luggage to arrive safely. Equip them with your Holy Spirit to guide them in everything they do and say. Let the love of Christ shine in their lives. We ask all these things in Jesus' name and for his sake."

Everyone joined him with a unified "Amen".

Some of the group members went toward the pastor to embrace him. Others picked up their carry-on luggage.

"Let's move on out!" Devonte' cried.

Everyone grabbed his or her belongings and we moved towards the security screening area. Now the fun begins. We went through separate lanes and prepared to go through the machines, metal detectors, and wands.

"Please have your ticket in your hand," a female security officer said in an authoritative manner. "Please have your boarding passes ready and your identification out."

We looked like cattle herded across the plains as we navigated through the security area. Like robots, we placed our belongings on the conveyor belts.

"Please remove your shoes, metal belt buckles, and keys from your pockets."

The looks on some of the faces around us were like sheep in their appearances. They seemed to be going through the lines without emotion. One woman was frustrated. She had to repeatedly return through the metal detector that sounded. They eventually moved her to the side and used a wand. People turned their eyes from her as not to appear to be associated with her (just in case something was found). There were persons dressed in business suits who seemed to effortlessly navigate through the lines as if they had done this hundreds of times before.

Being an experienced traveler, I was prepared. I placed all items that would potentially be questionable in my check-in luggage. The only inconveniences were removing my laptop computer and turning my cell phone on for the security personnel. I wore sandals and loosely-fitted comfortable clothing.

We all finally made it through the security area and rode the maglev to the airside of the airport. We arrived at Gate 14 a little over an hour since the time I entered the airport. I considered this more than a reasonable amount of time to make it to this point. I immediately looked for a place to plug in my computer. Others were on their cell phones, and some congregated into groups and pairs to talk. A couple of people went to sleep, while others viewed the television. There were a total of thirty-six of us. The individual goals of the members on the team may have varied, but the mission was the same for everyone – spreading the love of Christ.

"Excuse me Joshua."

I looked up from my computer at a smiling face. It was Ken. He was one of the members of the agricultural team. He would train people to grow a variety of crops. Most of the people are malnourished. They have a diet that is very high in starch. This is mainly potato products. The lack vital nutrients and minerals found in a variety of fruits and vegetables.

"What's up buddy?"

"We're headed over to the Café to get some coffee," he said. "Do you care to join us?"

"Thanks for offering," I replied. "But I have to complete a couple of things."

"No problem; I see you are busy."

"One more thing," I said. "When we get to Amsterdam, I'm buying."

"It's a date," Alex said. He was Ken's twenty-four year old son.

I was reviewing my writing, but I wasn't really paying attention to what I was reading. Even though it had only been a short period, I missed my family already.

"Flight 8371 for Amsterdam is now boarding our chairmen preferred and business class passengers. Also, persons traveling with children may board at this time."

I checked my ticket for my seat assignment. The team would not be sitting together. The pastor told Lawrence to purposely seat members of the team sporadically throughout the plane. He thought this would be a good manner in which to meet other travelers. The goal being that we would tell others about our mission trip, as it is natural to talk to the person beside you.

This would be a seven and a half hour flight. Even though I worked in children's ministry, I was hopeful none were around me on the plane. I finally boarded the plane and walked down the aisle looking for my assigned seat. When I finally made it to my row, a younger woman was already seated in the aisle seat. I sat at the window in order that I may sleep with my head against it.

I politely greeted the woman and introduced myself.

"Hello," I said. "My name is Joshua."

"Hello Joshua," she replied. "My name is Susan. I am pleased to meet you."

She extended her hand in friendship. I shook her hand and smiled. I removed my slippers from my bag and changed my shoes. I also retrieved my notes for the conference. I figured I would review them during both legs of the flights. The flight from Amsterdam to Entebbe, Uganda was also seven and a half hours. I placed my carry-on luggage in the overhead compartment. Once that was completed, I excused myself and sat in my assigned seat.

"I wonder who our neighbor will be?" she asked pointing to the empty seat between us.

"Maybe the airline didn't sell a ticket for this seat," I said.

"Where are you headed?" Susan asked.

"I'm a Christian missionary on my way to Uganda."

"That's very interesting," she replied. "What type of work will you be doing there?"

"I am one member of a team of people from my church. We will be doing different ministries while we are over there. We have a well digging and medical team. People will be working with building and trades, while others will be working with pastors. I will be leading our children's ministry."

"That sounds exciting."

"Where are you headed?" I asked.

"My husband is on business in Holland. He is staying longer than expected, and he sent me a ticket."

"That was very nice of him."

"This is my first trip to Europe."

"Mine too."

"Well, I guess we can get through it together."

Surprisingly, the seatbelt sign was illuminated, and no one filled the seat next to us. The flight attendant made the general announcements, and we were preparing for our departure.

"This may be our lucky day," Susan said. "No one has come for this seat."

"I know what you mean," I replied.

I reviewed my notes several times during the flight. It was too early in the day to go to sleep. I viewed one of the in flight films to pass the time. We were served lunch and a snack during the flight. I got out of my seat a couple of times to stretch my legs. When I went to the back, I met one of our team members.

"How's the flight going for you so far Greg?"

"It's brutal man," Greg replied.

"One more to go after this."

"Don't remind me."

We both engaged in stretching exercises. The dull resonance of the plane's massive engines drowned out the other noises around us. I returned to my seat and reread my daily devotional *Life Focus New Testament*. No too long after, we were preparing to land.

"Please place your seat upright," the flight attendant remarked in a sharp tone as she walked up the aisle.

When we arrived inside the terminal, we had to move quickly to make our connecting flight. Fortunately, our next plane was departing a few gates from where we arrived. We moved with a purpose down the jetway and walked briskly through the terminal. When we arrived at our gate, the business class persons were preparing to board.

Devonte' approached an employee making the announcements at the gate.

"Hello," he said in a polite voice. "Our flight just arrived from the USA. Will our bags make it on this flight?"

"Yes, sir," she stated. "Generally, your luggage moves faster than you. We won't be leaving for about 20 minutes. Your luggage will be offloaded and should be placed on this flight."

"Thank you very much."

"You're quite welcome sir."

Even though she sounded very convincing, you could tell he was somewhat apprehensive. A bulk of our ministry depended on the contents in those bags. It would be very disheartening if we did not have the necessary items to effectively complete our mission. I recall the pastor praying that our luggage would arrive safely. However, he did not specifically pray that it would arrive with us.

Before long, we were on the plane and well into our flight. It was getting a little late, and I wanted to review my notes a final time before our arrival. However, the cabin lights were dimmed after dinner. I (or my body) decided that I should go to sleep. This would make the time pass much more quickly. Luckily, I had been able to obtain an exit row seat. This afforded me the opportunity to stretch my legs in front of me. I reclined my seat and placed the pillow on the window. I then wrapped my body in a heavy-duty paper towel given to me by a flight attendant, which she called a blanket. Before I knew it, I was asleep.

I was awakened by the voice of the captain. She informed us that we would be landing very soon. Shortly after the announcements, the lights in the cabin were illuminated. What once was a serene dimly lit cave became a brilliantly enlightened beehive. The passengers moved about the aisle. The flight attendants were distributing hot hand towels.

Everyone was instructed to take their seats and secure their seatbelts. The decent of the airplane was now quite evident. I gazed out the window to view dusk that was throughout the land. What was only an idea in the mind on an individual and the vision of a mere mortal had now come into fruition. Joshua Hopkins had finally come home to Africa.

There was no jetway to meet the plane at the Entebbe airport. The plane landed near the terminal. Steps were placed at the door just beyond first class seating. The instant that I walked off the airplane two elements was quite evident. Humidity embraced my face at once when I broke the space between the door of the airplane and the outer surface. The next immediate sensation that invaded my senses was the smell of burning. I could not decipher if it was the smell of wood or something else. The passengers walked across the tarmac and filed into the building.

On the other side of the customs desk were the conveyer belts. I could see some of the team members congregated. As I was waiting in line, I removed the insect repellent from my fishing vest. It contained 100% deet as instructed in a meeting. I sprayed some on my hands and wiped all exposed skin. I then sprayed some on my clothing and waited patiently in line.

"Passport and papers please," the customs officers requested.

I surrendered my passport and entry visa. The officer looked at my passport and then me. He immediately stamped both documents and directed me to move through the metal detectors.

"Grab all the suitcases that have a red cross on them," Devonte' said.

"How was your flight?" asked Carol."

"Surprisingly enough," I added, "it was quite restful."

"I walked over to your seat to check on you, but you were asleep."

"I guess I was more tired than I thought."

We walked over to the others who were starting to take off some of the luggage from the belt. I know everyone was apprehensive about his or her luggage. Being in a third world nation was difficult in and of itself. We packed the very essentials in our carry-on luggage; however, our check-in bags contained a few comforts that would make the journey a little more bearable. The people standing around the conveyer were like fishermen. They were still, but the reality of bagging the big one was uncertain.

Bag by bag, we moved our luggage off the belt and into a corner. A sigh of relief overcame me when I sighted my personal luggage. I was glad that my team bag made it as well. However, that bag didn't contain my boxes of stowed away ginger snaps.

"Please take out your lanyards," Devonte' said. "Our mission begins here. From this point on, we are the Encounter Team. Let's take our baggage outside."

"What about my bag?" Jennifer asked.

"Roger, take her over to the baggage claim desk," Devonte' stated. "Give them this card; they can contact us once her bag arrives. We'll have a taxi that is coming from here to our site to bring your bag to us."

Jennifer didn't look too reassured from these words. I was hopeful that her bag would arrive on the next flight and be placed in a secure place. Unfortunately, every traveler is aware of the risks of unaccounted for luggage. Visions of your luggage being manhandled or worse the contents violated by baggage handlers were not comforting thoughts.

The safe return of her luggage would be one of the first miracles on the ground.

"Hello everyone," a voice yelled beyond the security gates.

It was Lawrence and the advance team members. We wearily greet them with embraces. For those of us in whom this was our maiden voyage to Africa, this was a soothing sight. Knowing that each of them had already been here one week safely was comforting.

"Welcome to Africa," Lawrence said with a smile. We are going to get into the vans and complete the final portion of this weary journey."

"Before we leave, I have a couple requests," Ivan said. "Make sure you use your seatbelt and lock your doors. None of the vans have air conditioners, so you will have to open your windows. Do not extend your arms or any other body parts out of the windows."

"Before we leave," Greg said, "how long is the drive?"

"The drive would be approximately four and a half to five hours," Ivan replied. "We will stop a few times for breaks."

"Okay everyone," Ivan said, "let's get moving."

As we drove out of the airport, I noticed a large lake at the edge of the property. It was a striking body of water juxtaposed to the airport. There were a few people in the distance at the edge of the water. Overhead, planes flew across the water and landed. There were a few people at the edge of the water. No vessels were on the water, although it could easily accommodate a host of them.

When our convoy arrived on the main road, I noticed that we were driving on the left side. This was quite awkward from my far western vantage point. There were seven of us in the van in which I was riding. There was also a police officer who had an AK-47 with the magazine attached. He sat in the front bucket seat to the left of the driver. It was somewhat menacing to have him in the van with us. However, the reality of our situation and the current climate of the country dictated that he be there.

While I knew that I was not alone in the van, my attention was on the events transpiring on the outside of my window. It was as if I had been transported back in time hundreds of years into Biblical days. There was much to digest and my eyes were never full. The sights were many as we moved about. The pace at which the convoy was moving would not allow me to slowly take in what I saw. I immediately retrieved my video recorder. I rested it on the ledge of the window. This would afford my family to see what I could in no way describe.

The streets of Kampala were bustling with people, bikes, and dusty vehicles. There did not appear to be any recognizable road etiquette. Men on bikes (that appeared to be decades old) darted between traffic. The bikes were either mopeds or peddle. On the back of these bikes was usually another person. The people who piloted the bikes were known as "bota bota" drivers. For a few coins, people could pay these drivers to take them about the town. I learned from our driver, Roland, that this was one of the most common modes of travel. Although they were inexpensive to rent, it appeared to me that this was not the safest means of travel. However, men straddling the seat or woman sitting sideways embracing a package did not seem phased by the navigation methods of their driver.

The most common motor vehicle appeared to be vans. These particular types of vans I don't recall if I had ever seen before, except in a *National Geographic* magazine. They were indigenous to Africa. Inside of these vans were straps pretending to be seatbelts. The seats were metal benches with a thin canvas pad. There were three rows of seating, not including the two seats in the front for Roland and the police officer. The metal that was the frame of the van was very thin. Three roll bars were spread apart from the front to the rear of it. The engine roared, as the driver skillfully shifted and navigated the vessel.

As we drove along the streets, we came within inches of other vehicles and people. At times, I had to close my eyes in many near misses of pedestrians and other motorists. I learned something interesting about the windshields of these vans. There were various words taped in decorative letters at the top. Some were obvious advertisements for various products. They mostly all appeared to be for some name brand jelly. However, the overwhelming majority of them were references to God. Some said, "Trust God." Others made some reference to Jesus. My favorite was "God Is Able."

These vans were loaded with people. It became clear that these were some form of taxi. When we would come next to a van, we would stare at the occupants. They would either smile at us or be totally oblivious to our presence.

The outdated vehicles spewed thick clouds of black smoke from their exhaust pipes. Some of these vehicles were carrying goods, such as food, coal, or building supplies. The smell of diesel fuel was substantial and hard to inhale. However, after sometime, it appeared my body adapted to not only the smell, but the brutal heat that transformed the van into an oven.

The buildings around Kampala were plain and numerous. No architectural wonders leaped out at the gazing eye. They appeared to be functional at best. Most of the business establishments that lined the road appeared to be shed like structures. They looked somewhat like the common shed in one's backyard, except they were wide in length and made of concrete. One square piece of large wood on each side of the opening of the building made up the doors.

The outsides of these edifices were ordinary in appearance. There were no fancy advertisements or illuminating "OPEN" signs displayed. It was coated with a flat exterior paint. Typically, it was yellow or blue. The dust and fumes from passing traffic collected on the buildings, which dulled their outer shell. The merchants would have their wares displayed directly in front of their buildings. I assumed it was to entice perspective customers to venture inside. Everything from clothing to raw meat was congregated in front of these buildings.

The merchants were very savvy. They displayed their most appealing items as the centerpiece of their establishments. Every passing individual was a potential customer. They pleaded the case of their merchandise whenever someone was within hearing distance. With smiles and demonstrative body motions, they moved in on persons who demonstrated the slightest interest as well as those who did not.

"Alright everyone," Roland said, "we are stopping for a break."

We looked out the window and noticed in the grass the thin trees with flat tops on either side. The other vehicles in front were parked as well.

"Where's the bathroom?" asked Carol.

"Take your pick," I said pointing to various trees.

"Welcome to Africa," Derek laughed as he helped Carol out of the van.

The police officers appeared to set up a perimeter around the convoy. One was placed at the front and back of each end of the convoy.

"Drink water!" a voice shouted.

I had already drunk two bottles of water. I was dehydrated once a few years earlier. That landed me a stay in the emergency room with IV's in both arms. I vowed that would never happen again, especially someplace that may not have the best facilities to accommodate me. After my trip to the little missionary's room, I decided to retrieve my camera. I moved about the group with my video camera.

"Hey Arnita," I said, "say hello to your friends back home."

"Hello friends back home," she replied.

"How do you feel now that you are in Africa again?" I asked.

"I love it!" she exclaimed.

Arnita was the leader of the Adopt An Angel program. As a former pastor's widow, she has a heart for the angel of the church.

"Tell me Arnita," I said, "how did you get involved with the Adopt An Angel program?"

"On my first missionary journey to Uganda, I met many pastors who were experiencing hardships. One pastor could be responsible for 15 or more churches in his district."

"Why are there so many churches under one pastor?"

"Well, since the people are so spread apart, it would be impossible for them to congregate at one church. Remember, most of them have no transportation and many of them already walk hours to get to church already."

"Okay."

"The layreaders have to build these churches with bricks, grass, and sticks. Most of the churches are outside under a grass shelter."

"How close are these churches for the pastors?"

"Most of the churches are spread far apart. This means the pastors would have to walk for days to reach a particular church. The lucky ones have bikes to ride. None of them have cars and can scarcely afford to take a taxi."

"Are those bikes durable enough to ride on these Ugandan roads?"

"The bikes that we purchased on my second trip here five years ago are totally useless today," she said. "This was not due to abuse, but overuse."

"How do the pastors sustain themselves financially?" I asked.

"The diocese cannot afford to pay the pastor's salaries," she replied. "So, many of them have to go months without pay. This means they have to obtain their own food and build their own homes."

"That's amazing."

"Many of the pastors adopt the orphan children in their villages. This creates an additional hardship for a pastor who may have four or more children of his own."

"So what was your solution?"

"I developed a program for members of our church to 'adopt' a pastor through a monthly $40 contribution. This is half of the monthly salary of a pastor."

"How many pastors signed up for the program?"

"Currently, there are 372 pastors enrolled in the program. Only 47 have sponsors."

"Besides the obvious poverty and disease that you see everyday, what is the hardest part of this mission?"

"The hardest part of my job is to say 'no'."

"What do you mean?"

Arnita's eyes began to water, and she looked towards the ground.

"When on a visit, a pastor in a distressed situation asks. . . ."

She paused for a few seconds and wiped her eye. I turned off the camera and placed my arm on her shoulder.

"He and his wife are sitting in their home. The pastor asks me does he have a sponsor. I have to tell them no. It is a heartbreaking scene."

"So, what else do you do while you are here?"

"While I'm here, I visit as many of these pastors as I can," she said. "You must keep in mind that these men are spread out among a considerable amount of distance."

"How long does it take you?"

"It could take three or more hours to reach them on roads made by human travel."

"I also deliver any gifts sponsors have for their pastors," she added. "Mainly, I assess their needs and see what we as a church can do to help."

"Besides the people who have sponsored pastors, what has the church done to help?"

"The church has provided *Bibles*."

"Am I to understand that the pastors don't have a *Bible*."

"Surprisingly, many of them don't have a good study *Bible*," she said. "You have to keep in mind that while they are not in one of their churches, a layreader is in charge."

"What's a layreader?"

"This is a person that provides the sermons when the pastor is not there. They can serve communion."

"Can they marry couples?"

"They can't perform marriages or baptisms," she added. "That's generally why the pastor visits the churches to perform these ceremonies and check on the status of the members of the congregation."

"What else has the church provided for the pastors?"

"We have provided mosquito nets. The mosquito nets help to control the outbreak of malaria among the pastors and their families. One or two mosquito nets are donated to each family. At night, they wrap themselves in the net."

"Is there one person per net?"

"No. About two to three people are in a net. In some cases, the entire family shares one net."

"What do you believe is most important to the pastors?"

"Their family members are probably most important to them. The pastors have children for which they cannot provide the basic necessities such as food, clothing, water, and education. They are willing to suffer, but they hate to see their children suffer."

"That's incredible."

"Somehow, they manage to survive and move on."

I was speechless.

"Don't worry Joshua," she said, "you'll have a great time on your visit."

Arnita was referring to the Adopt An Angel visits that every team member was assigned. At least one day, each team member is required to go on an Adopt An Angel visit. Each team member will meet approximately four pastors and their families. I am sure it will be an eye opening experience.

"I'm sure I will," I replied. "I look forward to it already."

On my way back to the van, my camera's attention turned to Jim. Jim was excited about being in charge of the well digging team. He had come to Uganda for the past six years.

"Tell us something about what you do Jim," I said.

"Roughly 84% of Ugandans live in rural areas," he replied. "Almost 45% of those people do not have access to clean drinking water. This means that a nation of approximately 28 million people, approximately 10 million people daily have to pray for rain or drink polluted water."

"How does the Ugandan government help the people?" I asked.

"On occasion, the Ugandan government will drill boreholes in rural communities," he stated in a very serious manner. "The cost is about $10,000."

"Is this in American dollars or Ugandan dollars?" I asked.

"American dollars," he replied.

I placed the camera down and looked Jim directly in the face as he continued his explanation.

"Once completed, the government does not usually monitor water levels or provide maintenance. As a result, it is forgotten and pretty much abandoned. Also, groundwater is a better drinking source than surface water."

"Why's that?"

"The groundwater does not contain detrimental pathogens and normally does not need to be treated."

"Unfortunately, most of the groundwater contains iron, which has an unpalatable taste," he added. "In addition to its awful smell, the water stains skin, clothes, and containers. This makes it unattractive to Ugandans who resort to drinking diseased surface water."

"What's the result of this?"

"This results in death, especially for the young and elderly. Thankfully, some engineers at my company have developed a viable option."

"What is it?"

"For about one tenth of the cost of drilling a regular well (about $1,000 American dollars), our team uses a method to extract ground water. Once completed, the water is treated to remove the iron content and fetid aroma."

"Are there any Ugandans on this team with you?"

"The team consists of local Ugandans, who provide manual labor and technical assistance. The local Ugandans are trained on how to maintain the well and dig new ones."

"What else does your team do here?"

"The team also visits previous wells we dug in the past. We also repair wells dug and abandoned by the government.

Although Jim was a large strapping individual, he was gentle as a lamb and very humble.

"Okay let's move out!" Lawrence said.

"Hey Jim," I said.

"Yeah."

"Thanks for all you do," I replied.

I shook his hand and moved to the van.

After driving for a short period, our convoy ventured off of an asphalt-paved road and onto one covered with dirt. The second that the tires hit the road, the earth began to soar. The roads were composed of a reddish clay substance. We had the choice of closing the windows and suffer from exhaustion from the heat or be covered in red clay and inhale the contents of the road. We opted for the latter.

The roads were treacherous.

There was no signage, guardrails, mile markers, light poles, or rest plazas on these dirt roads. It appeared that as fast as you could drive was the speed limit. Deep long trenches (that appeared to have been made from tires in muddy conditions) were more ordinary than level straight-aways. The van crashed down into these channels and profoundly swayed the passengers of the vehicle. Like a ship's captain sailing a vessel through a sea storm, Roland (seated upright and tall) maneuvered our van over treacherous terrains and precarious pathways.

Slow huge trucks carrying packages and people spewed thick black clouds of smoke into our windshield and delayed the convoy. At every opportunity, the van drivers darted around them. The drivers were gracious to one another. They tooted their horns or flashed their lights as some form of signal to rival drivers. At times, the road was too small for even opposing vehicles to share. Submitting to the larger opposing vehicles was the rule of the road.

I felt more safe flying over Greenland 43,000 feet in the air guided by the hand of a mere mortal, than driving a few hundred yards on this access road. I feared for the lives of those who peddled their bikes on these roads. At the sound of an approaching vehicle, they stopped and walked their bikes to the side. Securing their cargo, they waited patiently until the danger had passed. The loud pounding noise of the drive made it impossible to have a conversation. We would simply point at something outside the window that we wanted to bring to another's attention.

Children on their way to school in their brightly colored uniforms moved off the road and faced the oncoming traffic. Older children held the arms of the younger. I recall Ivan stating that if a vehicle carrying foreigners hit someone, the residents will kill them – excluding their African counterparts. Although the foreigners were not driving, they would receive the speedy and deadly justice.

The ominous mountains extended for miles deep into the Congo. I wondered what type of extraordinary and noxious creatures made their homes there. The soft blue painted sky seemed greater here. I was in awe of the thick brawny clouds slowing making their exodus across the heavens. For a moment, I envied the majestic birds that soared the skies and surveyed the landscape.

There were many new and interesting sights along the road from Kampala to the rural areas. However, the most arresting were those of the people. I never tired of being a people watcher. They moved about methodically down the roads and in their villages. As a vehicle approached, the people immediately moved off to the side of the road and into the bush. It was somewhat comical to see small children who have been obviously trained to move at the sound of an approaching vehicle.

A common sight would be people carrying a large yellow container. It looked like a gas container, but probably carried about five gallons of water. Some locals had two or more containers strapped to the back of a bike. It was also interesting to see wooden boxes with bottles of Coca-Cola in them. The bottles were the small slender kind that apparently disappeared from America in the seventies and made their way to Africa.

For some reason, I could not recall what day it was as we continued. My attention was fixed on recording with my senses as much information as possible. Some women had children strapped to their backs and items in their hands. The head wraps of many of them were bright and beautiful. The range of colors seemed to extend beyond the color spectrum. Those persons stood out among their plainly clothed peers.

Though the people were clothed, the articles were some-what dingy in appearance. This was due to the dust on road that flew into their homes or rested on them as they walked miles for water. The further we moved from the city, the more despairing were the living conditions and those that dwelled therein.

The homes that were once made of concrete transformed into shacks with clay bricks for walls with sticks and grass for roofing. While in Kampala, shabby little restaurants with patio furniture inside the main seating areas were common eateries for the residents. Out in the rural areas, open fires under boiling pots appeared to be part of the landscape.

The women seemed to be the main workers of the community. Mile after mile, you could see them hauling water, carrying bags, and bending straight down in the fields. Most of them had children in their immediate vicinity. The closer we approached, the closer a child became one with his mother. Peeking behind her dress and intently looking at the row of vans, but dare not move from the arch of safety of his mother's touch.

The older children were particularly friendly. They waved from the fields as the vans passed by them. Some even ran towards the convoy smiling and jumping feverishly at the sounds of the horns. A few of the team members in the vans in front threw water bottles from the windows for the children. The children quickly collected them and waved continually until we could no longer see them in the distance. Roland informed us that not only do the children drink the water, but they have various other uses for the empty bottles.

Every mountain we passed seemed fresh and new. The residences of the people were similar, but different. The skin color of the strangers was the same, but their reactions to us were special. My mind would not grow tired of seeing a group of people patiently waiting at a well or a string of churches spread across the green lands. Various rural schools were imbedded in the colorful African terrain. On occasion, we were lucky enough to see the children at play as we passed. Without the fancy playground equipment or jungle gyms, they children enthusiastically engaged one another with smiles and laughter.

After much trepidation, much time, and much prayer, we finally were just outside of our destination – Hoima.

Nothing in the area looked remotely like western civilization. Not the colors, smells, or foliage reminded me of any of the places I traveled from West Point to the Mohave Desert in the states. It was quite evident in the roads, structures, vehicles, and lack of billboards.

The Imperial Guesthouse (where we stayed) seemed like a palace compared to the quarters around us. It was surrounded by a fifteen foot stonewall. At the gate were armed guards, who cleared each van that passed by their checkpoint. They were very simple and amiable in their duties. Once inside the gate, the vans parked directly across from the main entrance.

"Welcome home everyone," Lawrence said.

"If this is home, I'm running away," Chloe said in a joking manner.

Morgan came to Uganda with his father Karl. They would be working with the building and trades team. Their mission was to provided tools and training to young men who were apprentices in various areas, such as carpentry and masonry.

"Let's check into our rooms and meet back in the lobby area for dinner and then a brief team meeting in a few hours," Lawrence added.

"Can we shower and change before the meeting?" Morgan asked.

"That's what I'm doing," he replied.

After retrieving our luggage, I collected my key and went to my room. I was one of the fortunate three persons who had a single room. That's exactly what it was – a room. There was no era décor to speak of. There was a bed, a wall closet, and a bathroom. The bed reminded me of the one I slept in as an elementary school student. There was nothing fancy about its structure or design. Attached to the ceiling above the bed hung a mosquito net. It was tied in a knot and hung about twenty-four inches over the center of the bed.

The wall closet was probably the most purely functional piece of furniture that I have ever seen in any second hand store. A closer inspection revealed that it was hand made, stained, and painted. Inside was a metal rod with various types of clothes hangers attached to it.

The bathroom – Oh my. The tub was made of cast iron and free standing. A drain ran from it to an opening in the floor. A thin rubber shower hose was connected to the wall. There was neither a hot or cold facet. A large knob labeled "OFF & ON" was affixed just above the tub's spout. I would surmise that it was several inches shorter than the American style tub, but would be standard in most European countries.

There was a table with a basin on it. Over the table was a square shaped mirror about the size of a dinner dish. It was attached to a wire that hung from a nail. Folded on the table were two white washcloths and a towel. They were clean and neatly folded. I tried the light switch; however, it did not work. I recalled hearing in a meeting that it was not uncommon for power to be sporadic in this part of Africa. It could be off for several minutes or hours.

I thought it was a good idea to take advantage of this time alone. A much-needed shower to remove the road dust and unpacking my belongings seemed to be in order. I could not believe the amount of dirt that had accumulated on my clothes. We were told not to swallow the water in the shower; any consumption of it could possibly prove harmful. I packed four containers of hand wipes. I used them throughout the drive to Hoima. I was amazed at the brown contents that they collected from my face.

As I stood in front of the mirror, I used them to wipe off my face. I thought not to take a chance with any of the water entering my mouth. I folded my clothes neatly and placed them in a large garbage bag I brought from home. I am sure I would find a needy individual who could use them before my stay had ended. Heaven knows I saw many of them on the way here.

Nevertheless, I decided that I would give away all of the items I had to the Ugandan workers in children's ministry. It would be quite easy to simply hand out the children's clothes, my wife's clothes, and mine to any person I met on the road. For surely, all but a few that could be counted on one hand was living in abject poverty. However, I believed that those persons who volunteered as children's ministry workers here in Uganda should be compensated in some manner.

A startling fact in Uganda is that half of the nation's population is under the age of eighteen. That meant that there were many children in search of the love that only Christ could provide. Due to AIDS, disease, and other contributing factors, this was the state of the nation.

These persons held ENK clubs meetings each Saturday in their homes or at local churches. Some of them adopted many orphans who live around them. They knew first hand the needs of their communities and those personally in need. Who better than they could decide who best needed the items I had in hand? Persons who are in ministry should be rewarded for their efforts. These people always give and rarely receive. They provide for, but never are provided for.

They find it hard to accept, for they believe its okay to go without for the kingdom.

Although this is a gracious path to take, it is not sensible. It is not a failing to receive something in return for your service. Nor is it a sin to receive a gesture of thanks from a friend or stranger. As long as you are not maliciously abusing others through taking advantage of them, it is quite acceptable to taste the harvests of your labor of love from others.

As I stepped into the shower, I was quite aware that my entire body would be most susceptible to mosquito bites. Once I removed the deet, it was time for them to eat. The wall of defense would come down. It was now time for the greatest shower time since the invention of the nozzle and hose. There were many things that I wanted to bring back from the continent with the oldest civilization. Malaria was certainly not one of them.

A logical approach seemed to be the best method to cleansing my body. My body jolted to the cold burst of water as if it were tapped by a cattle prod. If it were not for remembrance of the scorching sun of the day, this would be unbearable. I washed my body from top to bottom with the camping soap. I observed brown water descend from it endlessly. It seemed no matter how much I scrubbed, the water emptied light brown.

I quickly exited the bathroom. Once dried, sprayed and dressed, I began to unpack a few items. These included a flashlight, reading material, and secure bottled items. I did not want any visitors (insect, animal, or human) in my belongings or bags, so clothing and other items would remain zipped and locked inside.

I did not perceive the need to incite temptation of any of the three. I have seen various bugs as small as a gnat and as large as my fist during my brief tenure here. None of them are captivating in flight, simply a menacing sight. What they carry, where they've been, and what purpose they have to the fragile ecological system in this portion of the rainforest belt is of no consequence to me. If they come near me or in my belongings, I'm taking them out. I will mourn their loss and attempt to move forward in my mission.

It would be quite inviting for a small reptile to make his new residence in my dark cool bag. Having the receipt in my drawer at home to prove both date and amount of purchase would probably not deter a snake from entering my bag. The windows were not sealed into the walls. There was more than ample enough room for an uninvited guess to enter at will. At this very moment I noticed a small lizard clinging to the wall – motionless. Since it did not seem to be a threat, I decided to name him Larry. I assumed that he would eat mosquitoes and other insects. However, I will bring his appearance to the attention of Lawrence.

Finally, one does not know the hardships and temptations people face. Emotionally healthy and typical humans have an innate sense of guilt when taking something that does not belong them. It is almost like an instinct not to knowingly touch what you know is not yours. For others, the threat of retaliation from the owner or law enforcement persons is another deterrent for them to remain morally minded. However, if a mother is brought before a judge for stealing food for her starving children, would not mercy and grace be warranted? An individual's situation could make him or her take on a characteristic that is foreign to them. Furthermore, they will find themselves in regrettable circumstances of survival.

Those persons in the guesthouse, who would clean our room, wash our clothes, prepare our meals, and are the guardians of our possessions while we were out performing ministry, were in desperate situations. It was a great temptation for someone who had next to nothing to take something from someone who appeared to have so much. However, this still does not make it right. If we are blessed to improve our lives and the lives of others, we should do so. No baby asks to be placed in a pitiable situation. We walk on the road we were placed. We cannot curse our road or covet others. Also, not to appear to parade my possessions, or tempt beyond what another could bear, seclusion in my secure bag was the best decision.

Once I secured my luggage, I placed my attention to the bed. Surprisingly, it had a blanket covering it. This would be almost synonymous with an air conditioner in a room in Greenland. When would I ever use this blanket? However, I yielded to their expertise. Perhaps the nights could be as cold as the days were hot. Based on the advice of previous team members, I brought packing tape to patch holes in the bed netting. This was to ensure insects could not slip inside. Once I unfurled the net, I draped it over the bed and tucked it under. I carefully scanned each area of the net and patched all holes upon discovery.

I heard knocking on the doors down the hallway and a voice accompanying them. As the person came next to my room, I recognized that it was Devonte'.

"Okay everyone, "he said, "it time for dinner and a very brief meeting in the lobby."

He knocked on my door longer than the others.

"Hey Joshua. Open up," he said.

I moved from my bed and headed to the door.

"What's up Devonte'?" I asked.

"I just checked in on you to let you know that Sarah called."

"That's great. What did she want?"

"She said she would meet you here after breakfast."

"Thanks for giving me the message."

"No problem."

"Let's go meet the others."

We walked down the hallway together and into the entrance hall of the guesthouse. There were some plastic tables and chairs in the area. Some of the team members were already seated and chatting with one another. They appeared to be seated in their team mission groups at the tables. Since I was a team of one, I decided to sit with Carol and the others. Carol, Sonsarae, and Dana were the three nurses who were the medical team.

"Ladies may I join you?" I asked.

"No," Sonsarae said jokingly, "this place is reserved for good looking men."

"Then why doesn't it have my name on it." I gave both Sonsarae and Carol a hug.

"Where's Dana?" I asked.

"She went back to her room to get some medication," Sonsarae said.

Sonsarae was just like her name – very unique. She was a pediatric nurse in the premature infant ward at Children's Hospital. She worked twelve-hour shifts and overtime when offered. She was sweet, single, and saved. This was somewhat of a rare find for someone at her age.

"I couldn't believe how dirty I was," I said, "when I was taking a shower."

"I bet," Sonsarae said.

"No matter how much I washed, the water still came off of me brown."

"That's because the water you are bathing in," Carol said, "is brown."

"No way," Sonsarae said.

The look on Sonsarae's face said it all for both of us. The guesthouse had no underground pipes leading into it. The water supply came from a large black tower at the furthest point at the edge of the property made of industrial strength rubber.

"Lawrence told me," Carol stated, "that last year lighting struck the tower and it split."

"Whoa," I said. "What did they do for water?"

"I don't know. But there weren't any showers for quite sometime."

"I'm glad they had that fixed before we came," Sonsarae said.

"That's why the advance team comes one week earlier than we do," Carol continued. "They make sure everything is as perfect and safe as it can be before we get here."

"Thank God for that," Sonsarae declared.

As we were talking, the guesthouse staff was placing covered containers on tables that were against the front wall. Sterno cans were lit and placed under the large silver food containers. It appeared that we would be eating buffet style. The plates and serving utensils were placed to the right of the food.

"It's time to eat everyone," Gwen said. "Let's gather around in a circle and pray."

With a smile on her face and beckoning hands, she herded us together. Gwen was Lawrence's wife. She was also from Australia. She was his safety net. Whenever minor details needed to be taken care of concerning the entire team, you could correctly assume that it was Gwen who took care of them. They were married over 31 years and were missionaries in South Africa, Mexico, and Bolivia. Just looking at the inviting smile of Gwen comforted you.

After a short prayer, we formed a line to be served dinner. Just as I approached the use of water cautiously, I had a more healthy respect for foreign meat and fruit. A couple of the team members in front of me piled their plates high with food. I was not going to take the same approach. I figured that it was probably safer to practice temperance it this situation. The further I could put off my inevitable meeting with the Ugandan toilet the better. If I was out and about, who knows what was waiting for me.

"Oli ota?" I asked.

"Ndi Kurungi," she said with a smile.

I learned a few phrases from the booklet given to us at one of the team meeting. This phrase meant: "How are you?" To which she replied, "I am fine."

"My name is Joshua," I stated. "What is your name?"

"I am called Mary," she replied.

"Hello Mary. What is this?"

I was pointing at the first item on the table. It was in a large round dish. The food was resting on two large palm leaves.

"It is matoke"

"What is that?"

"It is like a banana."

"But it looks like cooked yellow mashed potatoes."

"Yes. It is very good. You try some."

"Just a little please."

"What type of meat is this may I ask?"

"It is beef."

"Just a little please. I'll have some vegetables thank you."

I grabbed a couple of rolls and a pat of butter. As I moved further down the table, there were glass pitchers filled with what appeared to be mango juice. I observed that others were drinking it, and I assumed it was safe to do so. I poured some in a glass and went to my table.

As I walked towards my table, I looked to the left and noticed some children walking down the road. I wondered what they would be eating tonight, or if they would be eating at all. I felt somewhat guilty for turning my nose at food that anyone on that road would have thankfully taken.

When I returned to my table, the ladies had already begun to eat.

"Is that all your having?" asked Carol.

"You're going to waste away here," Sonsarae added.

"I packed some treats in my bag back in my room," I said.

"Well," Carol added, "I hoped you packed a lot."

"So Carol," I said, "exactly what are you going to do while you are here as the person in charge of the health team?"

"We are going to distribute the book entitled, *Where Women Have No Doctor: A Health Guide for Women.*

"That sounds like a very interesting book. I can already tell from the title what it is about."

"Who receives a copy of this book?"

"We decided that this would be an excellent book for the women."

"Especially for those in the smaller villages," Sonsarae added.

"We travel to various rural areas and conduct seminars. We train women to become leaders and use what they have learned in the meetings to train others."

"That's great."

"It is our intention to train them how to effectively use this book and take this knowledge back to their homes and villages."

"How is that?"

"We are going to take some of the ailments and injuries that are most common to this area and focus on those. For example, burns, STD's, contusions, and broken bones."

"This sounds fascinating."

"That's only one thing we are doing. We also teach about aspects of childbirth, breastfeeding as well as post and prenatal care."

"Don't forget about health and nutrition," Sonsarae said.

"We are hopeful that once they get back to their homes, they will train someone else how to use this book. These women are so far away from any type of medical help that death is usually the result of something that could have been taken care of so easily."

"You are doing a great work. I am sure this will save countless lives."

"Carol you didn't mention the first aid kits," Sonsarae said.

"Oh yeah," she added. "We have first aid kits to distribute."

"That sounds great."

"We don't have that many. We only have about thirty or forty kits."

"Space was an issue," Sonsarae said, "as you know." "Besides, the government was taxing us so heavily that it would be cheaper to purchase the first aid kits here in Uganda."

"We will probably purchase some in Kampala," Carol added.

"Once the women are trained, we will come back to assess their needs. Of course we don't have enough money to supply all their desires. However, we can help them a little bit here and there."

"Sonsarae," I asked, "are you involved in the training as well?"

"Not at all."

"What are you doing?"

"Dana and I were trained on how to use a machine that reads the prescription on eyeglasses. We are going to fit people for eyeglasses."

"You know, I am glad that you mentioned that," I said. "That is the one thing that I could not put my finger on while I was here. I knew that there was something different about these people. No one is wearing eyeglasses. I'm sure there are some people who need them."

"Yeah. Even if they knew they needed them, none of them could afford to purchase them," Carol added.

"I remember in tenth grade sitting in the back of United States History class. I could not read the board. I had to move up to the front. Even though I told my mother I could not see well, she never took me for an eye exam. It was not until I went to the Army that I received my first pair of glasses. I went three years in high school squinting trying to get a clear picture."

"Unfortunately," Sonsarae said, "most of these are reading glasses."

"That is an excellent start," I said.

"As you may recall, we had people donate glasses at the church. This machine will read the prescription on the glasses, and we will fit someone with them."

"I remember when I received the gift of sight with glasses. It was a blessing to be able to see things clearly. I can imagine the joy these people will feel when they are able to see faces, even the faces of their children clearly for the first time."

"What a wonderful blessing that will be," Carol said.

"I wish I could be there to see it," I added. "It will be great to actually be able to read something without holding the book right on your nose."

"Maybe you can," Sonsarae said. "What are you doing Thursday morning?"

"I will be at one of the schools in town at any given point of that day. I am expected to meet about 3,500 children each day.

"That's a lot of children," Carol said.

"Take pictures of the seminars and bring them back to share with the members of the team. What will Dana be doing this week?" I asked.

"A few years ago, the church started a clinic," Carol said. "It's been hard trying to find a full time nurse – let alone a doctor. Dana will be helping them organize the medications that we sent. This will be especially true for persons who need malaria medication."

"What percentage of people do you think have malaria?" I asked.

"More than half I would imagine," she answered.

"I am sure it's probably close to 100% in the rural areas and villages," Sonsarae said.

The conversations we had as time progressed at the table were normal and everyday. We discussed the flight on the plane, the drive on the roads, and most importantly our rooms. It was very soothing to be with a group of people who shared your values, beliefs, and concerns. This made the time away from our families and the lack of the comforts of home a little more bearable. For many of us, this would be our first night on the Dark Continent. However, I knew that this would be a most memorable experience for everyone. Already, I felt that I knew a lot about the people around me and those sitting at this table. I knew that once we would return to America, our friendships would continue.

When it appeared that everyone had apparently finished dinner, Lawrence stood in the middle of the room and made an announcement.

"Let's move these tables out of the way and form a circle with these chairs," Lawrence requested.

Some moved tables to the far wall. Along with others, I began to form a circle in the center of the room. Once the deed had been done, we sat down and began our meeting.

"First, I want you to know that we contacted Pastor John," Lawrence said. "He will personally let our families know that we have arrived safely. Before we officially begin, let me start with a brief introduction," Lawrence said.

He turned to an older African man who was seated next to him. He placed his arm on the gentleman's shoulder and smiled.

"Some of you have already met this young man," Lawrence said. "He is no stranger to us. This is Bishop Frederick Byabajunga. He is the retired bishop of the

Bunyuro-Gitara Diocese, which is where we are currently ministering. He will be our spiritual leader while we are here in Uganda."

"And friend," Bishop Byabajunga added.

"Quite right," Lawrence said. "And our friend. Please welcome Bishop with a great big God bless you."

As on cue, everyone looked in the direction of the bishop and did so. The bishop seemed like a simple and humble man. He did not seem to be overconfident with his title or vain about his position in our group. As he personally distributed a hymnal to each group member, he began to speak.

"Good evening everyone," he said.

"Good evening."

"Welcome to Uganda. You are in the Bunyuro-Kitara Diocese. This is the oldest kingdom in Africa. It dates back over 3,000 years. And if this is your first time here, welcome to Africa. I want to begin with a brief prayer before we begin our service. I know Lawrence likes to call them team meetings, but they will be services here. Is that okay?"

"You're in charge bishop," Lawrence said. "Do as you are led by the Holy Spirit to do so."

"Thank you very much. I am going to ask everyone to pray. You all have many many missions to accomplish here. Those of you who have been here before have a good idea of what to expect. For those of you that this is your first time here in Africa, you have no idea what to expect. But, God does. Thank you for coming to help your brothers and sisters in the Lord. Now, I ask that we observe a moment of silence so that you can pray for God to empower you to complete the great task set before you."

The room became silent. Even the workers stood still and lowered their heads. You could hear nothing. I have prayed and prayed so many times up until this point. I didn't know what else to pray for at this moment. I heeded the bishop's advice and asked God to give me guidance and direction. Then, the bishop began to pray.

"Most gracious God, we ask that your mercy would be extended to us. Touch these here your people in a special way. Give them wisdom and courage to complete their mission here in Africa. We thank you for allowing them to come here safely and ask that you would continue that favor until they return home to their loved ones. Let Your Holy Spirit comfort and empower them. Lord God, you know our schedules, plans, appointments, and programs. However, if there is a greater need that needs to be met Lord, send me. We ask this all in the great wonderful beautiful and perfect name of Jesus. Amen."

"Amen and amen," Lawrence said. "Let's begin our devotions with a little song I would like to teach you. It is less than ten words. Every person in the area knows this song. They begin their meetings, school day, and special events with this song. I will say the words and then give you the translation. Better still. . . Bishop."

"I am here sir."

"Could you please give us the words to Tukutendereze Yesu?"

"I would be most honored."

"Thank you sir."

"The words are as follows. Tukutendereze yesu. Olimwana gw'endiga. Omusayi gunazeza. Nkwebasa omulokozi. Now sir, will you please give these people with confused looks on their face the translation"

"I would be honored," Lawrence said. "This song simply says, 'Let us praise Him, his name is Jesus. Jesus is the lamb, the Son of God. Jesus shed His blood and washed me. Thank you O my Savior.'"

"Do you have a cheat sheet I can borrow?" Sonsarae asked.

The room erupted in laughter.

"Don't worry my friends," the Bishop said. This song is in our devotional book. You will not learn this tonight, but by the time you leave from Uganda you will have both this song and the people in your hearts."

After we sang our devotional songs, the Bishop gave us a brief history on the region in which we resided. He gave us stories of bravery and poverty as well as heroics and hardships. From my numerous correspondences, research, and discussions with others, I felt that I really knew these people. They would not be distant strangers, but lifelong friends I have yet to meet. The meeting concluded with Ivan's safety briefing.

"Alright everyone, before you go to bed, please check your vehicle assignments posted on the wall of the guard shack. I will knock on your doors each morning at 6:00 a.m. Breakfast will be served at 7:00 a.m. Depending on what you are doing, you will either have lunch delivered to your location or a brown bag lunch will be placed in your vehicle. Have a good evening and lock your doors and use your mosquito nets."

After a few brief "hellos and good-byes" I went directly into my room. I wanted to review my notes for tomorrow and wind down the day. When I entered the quiet room, I immediately took off my clothes and dawned my sleeping gear. It consisted of the following: pajama pants, a long sleeve rayon shirt, socks, and a sleeping cap. This may seem to be a bit much, but in this environment, there is no room for error.

Even preparing for bed was a production here. I inserted my toothbrush in a bottle of water in order to make the bristles soft. This was the only way to brush, since we couldn't use the water in the tub. It took two bottles of water to brush my teeth. I felt bad using water in this way in a place where clean water is a commodity. However, for my safety, it had to been done this way.

Once under the mosquito net, I tucked it under the mattress. Under the netting with me were my conference notes and flashlight. I also had a snack size pack of chocolate chip cookies to supplement tonight's meal. I read these notes so many times that the words were running together. I had the content knowledge, but could I convey this information in a palatable manner to an entirely different culture of people? My extensive speaking career spanned from pre-Kindergarten to the postgraduate level. However, it remained in the continental United States – until now.

Insects (either attracted by my light or electric personality) were buzzing around the room. A few landed on my netting.

The room was entirely quiet. Besides the chirping of insects outside of the room, the noise of me breathing is the only sound that could be heard. I grew up in a crowded home. My current residence consisted of a wife, three active children, and uninterrupted calls and visitors. Our home is constantly filled with sounds from people, electrical equipment, or street noises. But right now, where I lay was totally silent. No voices, television, or neighbors dogs. Nothing. Just for a brief instant, I felt totally alone.

Yes, I was aware that there were others in the guesthouse with me. But under that netting, reading by the illumination of a flashlight in the dark, I was alone. Precious would not encroach upon my personal space in the middle of night. Jr. or one of the twins asking for breakfast would not awaken me.

Alone and under this net for the next thirteen days would be my home.

I did not sleep much during the night season. Restless-
ness could describe what I experienced last evening. As
time progressed, a flake of light leached in from a crack in
the door. I sat in bed and stared into what was almost entire
darkness. I do not know how much time passed – possibly
two or three hours. I heard Ivan walking down the hallway
knocking on the doors.

"Good morning," he said.

Three times, he wrapped his knuckles on the door. After
every set of knocks, he would repeat the same thing. I heard
one door open and a couple of voices. However, I could not
make out what they were saying. I moved onto my knees
into the praying position. Tired from a lack of sleep, I knew
that I had to get up from where I lay. Today, it was not about
me.

I emerged from under the net and onto the floor. Once I
found the lamp in my room, I was pleased to find out that it
was working. I opened my luggage and selected my clothing
for that day. It would be simple serve its purpose. I used
hand-wipes to clean my face and neck.

I was the second person out for breakfast that morning.
Christine was at a table drinking a cup of coffee. I went to
the tables where the food was located. I served myself some
eggs, jelly, and toast. I brought a bottle of water from my

room to drink with my breakfast. Lawrence arranged that a case of bottled water would be placed in everyone's room.

"Good morning Destiny."

"Good morning Joshua."

Destiny was the founder of One Child. It was an orphanage she and her husband began. They cashed in a $17,000 savings bond that they had for quite some time and built an orphanage in Hoima. She started the One Child sponsorship program at our church. It works similarly to the Adopt An Angel program.

Once in a while, a flyer is placed in the bulletin explaining the program. I cannot quite recall all the details. However, I do remember that for about $30 a month, you can sponsor an orphan. The children are rescued from the streets and placed in the orphanage under the guardianship of caring adults.

"How did you sleep last night?" I asked.

"Not too well," she replied.

"I know what you mean. It's hard getting used to a new bed."

" – And a new environment."

"Definitely."

"What are your plans for today?"

"Well, I am giving a seminar to some people who would like to start children's clubs in their neighborhoods."

"Oh yes. I remember you telling us about. . . what was it. . ."

"ENK-U clubs."

"Yes, that's it."

"This week, we will visit approximately fifteen schools"

"That's remarkable."

"What are your plans today?"

"Well, I plan to visit as many orphans as I can."

"I thought the orphans were staying in the home you and your husband constructed."

"Yes. Some of them do."

"Where are the rest of them?"

"Well some of them are with pastors. Others have had both parents die, and they live with a relative or a family in the village or town."

"So how many orphans are there?"

"Currently we have 88 orphans who are adopted by my friends, relatives, or members of our church."

"How many orphans total do you have?"

"We have approximately 450 orphans waiting to be adopted. We have to turn them away from our doors everyday. Sometimes, babies are found on our doorstep in the morning. Most of them have died in the night waiting for us to find them in the morning."

"That's terrible."

"We try not to turn away babies. So we made a box that someone places the baby in at night. An alarm sounds to let the workers know that a baby has been placed in the box. We try to find a local family who can take care of the child until we find a sponsor who can adopt him or her."

"How do you pay the workers? Does a portion of the money go to pay the care takers at the orphanage?"

"No. My husband and I pay their salaries out of our own money."

"Some of the money goes to maintain the maintenance of the building. Also, a portion goes to provide food and very little clothing."

"Where does most of the money go to?"

"Medical care and school fees. As you know, education is not free here. My husband and I believe that the way to help get these children out of poverty is through a healthy body and mind."

"Without exception, every one of these children is suffering from some type of medical ailment. Some have AIDS. All but a few do not have malaria from sleeping outside or in horrendous conditions. Some have extreme medical conditions. However, the majority of them are simple maladies that could be taken care of with over the counter medicines."

"Can we provide this for them?"

"First, there are no stores or hospitals to obtain the drugs. The clinic provides us with what they can. And if there were, we could probably not afford to purchase enough to take care of all their concerns."

"Even if you stopped paying the school fees?"

"Even if we stopped paying the school fees? Most (if not all) of the children who attend school has some form of medical concern."

"Yes, I remember what Ivan said about the AIDS epidemic in this region."

"Well, it's true. AIDS and malaria are rampant here. They cope the best way they can and move ahead with their lives."

"You're doing a great work here in Africa."

"I don't feel that I am doing enough."

"What do you mean?"

"There are hundreds of orphans that need to be adopted. Most of them we don't know who they are."

"But you have adopted some."

"Only 88."

"That is eighty-eight times a thousand."

"What do you mean?"

"Every year, the Muckleshoot Indian Tribe monitors the numbers of salmon that migrate from the ocean to Lake Washington. They enter through the Hiram M. Chittenden Locks."

"So what does this have to do with my situation?"

"I'll tell you. I was camping with a friend near Lake Washington. While we were fishing there, a man walked by and told us this story. One year, a young father and his son went on an overnight trip. On their morning walk, they came upon a school of salmon that were collected in a basin. The salmon must have been thrown into it by the waves, which had subsided by this time. Although the fish attempted to jump out of the basin and into the flowing water, their efforts were futile. The father knew that it would not be long before hungry bears would come and devour the fish. The bears may even challenge the two of them, which made every second that they were there more dangerous."

"So what happened?"

"The father knew that the survival of the salmon may have been riding on the hundreds of fish trapped in the basin. Each fish represented thousands of potential eggs. Only a few of the fertilized eggs become full grown salmon that return home. Unfortunately, he could not reach them because of his size. However, the son knew he could. Seeing the desperate situation of the salmon, the son went down into the basin, which had become filthy from many dead fish and runoff from the land."

"What did the boy do?"

"One by one, he threw the fish out of the basin and safely into the river. When he was doing so, he cut his leg under the waterline on the rocks. His blood spilled among the fish. The boy or the father was not aware of the injury. As the fish swam safely away, they never looked back as if to thank the child. Not long after, a large bear approaching was spotted by the father. He had only seconds to pull his son out of the basin and escape to safety."

"Please don't tell me the boy was killed by the bear."

"No. His father was able to safely pull him out and escape to safety."

"Thank God."

"Unfortunately – "

" – I knew there was more."

125

"The boy did not know how badly he was injured. However, the father knew. By the time the father was able to get the boy to a medical facility he died."

"What was the cause of his death?"

"Severe hemorrhaging."

"That's awful."

"In that area today, I know that just over 400,000 return every year."

"That's amazing."

"At one time, they were almost totally wiped out. However, thanks to the son who gave his blood, they thrive today not knowing who it was who gave his life for them."

"That's amazing."

"I don't know if the man's story about the father and son was true. However, I do know that from those 88 children, possibly thousands will now live in eternity in heaven. You will never meet them until one day in heaven. One day in heaven, thousands of people will be in a line waiting to give you a hug. Your sacrifice to save someone who was their relative or friend led them to the saving knowledge of Christ. These children will have children, and they will have friends who will have families. You don't know how many thousands of people will hear of their salvation, which began with a parentless child at a small orphanage in Hoima."

"Thanks Joshua for sharing breakfast with me."

"No, it was my pleasure."

Before we knew it, more people came out to eat. It was time for our day to begin. Talking with Destiny not only encouraged her, but me as well. As I turned about, I saw Ivan standing with someone and pointing at me. I knew immediately that it was Sarah. We sent pictures of our families to each other months ago through e-mail. I walked towards her smiling face.

"Hello Sarah."

"Hello Salongo. We finally meet."

Salongo is Bunyuro for father of twins. This was the nickname that was given to me by her. I gave her a hug and invited her to breakfast. She declined and said that the persons participating in the seminar were waiting for me at the church. We took the vehicle assigned to myself and headed for the center of town. The guard that was assigned to our van sat in the front passenger seat.

"So, how was your flight?" Sarah said.

"Very long," I replied.

"Thank you for the materials you sent to me."

"You are quite welcome."

"Did you receive all my notes for the seminar today?"

"Yes, I did."

"Do you think that there will be any problems with the participants understanding them?"

"No, I do not believe."

"So, there will not be any translation problems."

"Everyone who is participating in this seminar must speak English well. The children in their clubs may have to be spoken to in another language. But, to participate in this training, you must be able to read and speak English."

The town of Hoima had very little space that would be conducive to hold many seminars. Also, there were so many groups that needed the little space available. I decided that the church sanctuary would be fine to hold our seminar.

"The church is only a few minutes away," Sarah said.

Driving through this region on various roads at a good rate of speed was one thing. Now, the pace we traveled permitted me to see in more detail the lives of these people. The market place was bustling with people and vehicles. The people were as divergent as the types of products that decorated the storefronts. Some were fully dressed with long sleeves, pants and ties. Others wore tattered shirts and pants with no shoes. There were women with long braids down their backs, while others' heads were completely shaved.

The homes were small and discolored. Foliage was rampant around them. They were sporadically placed throughout the town. In retrospect, there was not really a distinctive mark between were the residential area began and where the commerce area ended. They were intertwined. It appeared that people built homes where there was space available. It would not be uncommon to see a place of business, a home, and a group of cattle grazing within ten feet of each other.

Another salient feature was the litter. From the guesthouse to our current location were endless trails of trash. It saturated the streets and adorned the fronts of businesses and residential dwellings. It consisted mainly of paper products. Discarded and ignored, it was pushed to the edge of the roads by the force of the wind or speeding vehicles. The lush flourishing African flora juxtaposed against the discolored decomposing waste was needles to my eyes.

"We are here," Sarah said.

"What a spectacular church," I replied. "Is this where you attend?"

"Yes. We have two services here on Sunday. This first service is in English and the second service is in Bunyuro – the local language."

"About how long are the services?"

"Each one is approximately three hours."

As we neared the threshold of the main entrance, we could hear the sounds of people singing, hands clapping, drums beating, and tambourines playing. It was a sweet sound that I have never heard before. I have seen people from this region sing on television. As a live witness, I can testify that the greatest fiber optic network could not transmit the spirit and heart of the music that inundated this house of God. It provided me with the needed burst of energy from last evening's lack of sleep. It was better than any multivitamin and more exuberating than a brisk power walk through the park.

There were no lights in the sanctuary. Nor was there glass in most of the windows. The light of God (provided by the sun) illuminated this massive gothic edifice built by hand decades ago. As I walked towards the pulpit, I noticed the hand carved wooden pews perfectly aligned from the rear to the front. The ceiling extended to the steeples of the church. This enhanced the harmonic sounds that now reverberated off the walls.

As I walked past the vibrant group of singers they offered a warm smile in my direction. I returned the gesture. Sarah placed me a chair facing the group. It consisted of approximately fifty persons. Most of them were young women. I could not contain myself as they continued in song. Like the man at the gate beautiful in Acts 2, I arose leaping and praising God. The African trait inside of my DNA was aroused, and I joined them in song and dance.

What happened in that meeting began a change in me. I met new lifelong friends on this occasion. I shared with them what was on my heart for the children of Africa. As I spoke during one of my lectures, the primary school located directly across from the backyard of the church had dismissed the children for recess. As on cue, the laughter and adolescent sounds that know no cultural boundaries overshadowed my voice. These children provided the backdrop to my message that day and the passion of my purpose for eternity.

At the end of the workshop, eleven members from the group (including Sarah) and I stayed after to discuss the plans for the upcoming days. We made arrangements to visit fifteen schools that week. We would visit five schools each day. The purposes of these visits were to recruit children and inform them of the ENK-U clubs. The members of the seminar who would accompany us lived strategically throughout the area. We would attend schools located close in proximity to their homes. This would ensure a strong attendance at the club meetings.

Sarah provided me with a letter delivered to the principals at their schools on the diocese's stationary. She also decided that we would spend one day in the town of Masindi. The following was a letter to five schools there we would visit:

Bunyuro-Kitara Diocese
Church of Uganda

The Head Teacher,
Kalalega P/S
Kyema P/S
Walyoba P/S
Karujubu P/S
Katasenywa P/S

May 10, 2008

Dear Sir/Madam:

RE: Visit to your school for children's ministry on Wednesday, May 21, 2008.

I greet you in the precious name of our Lord and Saviour Jesus Christ.

The purpose of this letter is to inform on the above subject.

I'm glad to inform you that your school is among the chosen few which will be visited in the Diocese.

You will be visited by Joshua who comes from the United States, and he will be accompanied by other members to do children's ministry in your school.

Your school will be visited on May 21 between the hours of 1:00 p.m. – 3:00 p.m.

We look forward to meeting you.

Yours in the Lord's vineyard,

Rev. Sarah Rubelema
Children's Ministry Coordinator

CC: Bishop Bunyuro-Kitra Diocese
Bishop Masindi Diocese
Diocesan Secretary
Diocesan Education Secretary
Principal Education Officer
American Children's Ministry Coordinator

We decided that the best manner to approach these visits was a large group presentation by me after a period of praise and worship. It was surprising to learn that the public schools in Africa encouraged visits by Christian groups. In fact, I was informed by Sarah that when other school administrators learned that their schools were not included in the visit, they became quite saddened. They sought how they could to be placed on our agenda. Sarah informed them that I would not be visiting them this week; however, the local ENK-U club leaders would visit them with a presentation prior to the end of the month. This was satisfactory to them, even though they would have liked their children to have seen the brown man from America.

I was told that my presence would have a lifelong influence on the people I met. Sarah told me that my presence at the schools would "challenge" the child to do well. Many people passed by the front of the church on their way to other destinations. The skin of the people in this region was very dark. When they saw a dark skinned person, they understood that person to be an African. When they saw a white skinned person, they understood that person to probably be an American, but most likely a European. When they saw me, they had no idea what I was. Whenever some people saw me, they would point and speak in Bunyuro. I asked Sarah what they were saying.

"Sarah," I said. "What is it that the people are saying about me?"

"Let me explain it to you this way," she said. "Mujungu means White man. Bujungu means Black man. Some people, but especially the children, are somewhat confused when they see you."

"Confused by what?"

"You may hear them say 'Mujungu randiki Munua'."

"What does that mean?"

"In our language it means, 'Is he a White man really?'"

"Then, what do they say?"

"Well, some argue that you are a White man. Look at his skin. Then, the others say no, he is a Black man look at his hair."

"Then, they compromise and say, 'Mujungu akwisau munya – Uganda.'"

"And what does that mean?"

"It means that you were probably born in Africa. Then, you later went to Europe and came back. So, I would say it means a Ugandan returned from another country."

"So, I guess they believe something happened to my skin when I left the country."

"Yes. You are correct."

As we traveled to different schools sharing our love and the gospel message of Jesus Christ, I grew even more connected with the group that we called ourselves Ikumi Na Ibri or The Twelve. We purposely made our traveling group twelve members. I explained to Sarah in one e-mail that if the twelve disciples could change the face of the world, then we could change the direction of a nation. Prior to my arrival, a number of potential ENK-U club leaders had a desire to visit with me at various schools. However, Sarah, through prayer and observation, selected the ten persons to serve on our children's ministry team.

From school to school, the children were fascinated and grateful of our presence. Some of the children would scream and run when I had my puppet lurch at them. They quickly picked up on the beat I played with my harmonica. When it came time for instruction, they listened intently. We decided that a translator would be best, especially for the very young children. Thousands of children and adults gave their lives to Christ and to His service. Some rededicated their lives and promised to live as a light in a dark world.

We were even invited to two Muslim schools. Both schools were located in Muslim neighborhoods. It was somewhat intimidating as the neighbors (out of curiosity) would congregate outside of the fences around the school. This request to come to these schools was not by any member of our team, but the request of the teachers and children. Some of the children at these schools came from Christian homes and areas around the town. Most of the schools are boarding schools. Consequently, the children are separated from their families and friends for quite some time.

The headmasters are understanding in this area and were quite open to us presenting at their schools. We were permitted to invite the children at these two Muslim schools to come to Christ. Over 500 of them accepted the invitation. Each of the two headmasters in turn would permit our team to return to the schools on a weekly basis to disciple the children. This was truly a great miracle.

At one school, two girls presented me with four eggs. I was later told they learned that I was coming to their school months in advance. As a result, they wanted to do something nice for me. That morning, their family decided to abstain from breakfast and give me the eggs that they would have eaten that day. I was in no position to accept such a great sacrifice. Lucky, a small church neighbored the school, and I gave them to the pastor and his family. He was quite grateful and invited us in to lunch.

I had forgotten the African tradition that whenever someone comes into your home, you must prepare a meal and drink. In most cases, the cost to prepare a meal for us would be a month's income of a family. Not only did they have to feed me, but the other eleven, our police officer, and the driver of our van. Luckily, I remembered that you could decline a meal and simply place ashes from the fireplace on your lips. This was also a tradition at each school we visited. After our presentation, we would be invited into the headmaster's office to sign the visitors log and dine on sweet crackers and bottled water.

Each evening, the group would return me to the guesthouse first. The guards at the gate recognized us by our loud praising in song, which could be heard well before we reached our destination. Even the police officer assigned to our van (Stephen) was affected by our group. He shared how he had children at one of the schools and could we visit them. I had a rule that any request by a person with loaded AK-47 would be honored. On the last day, we visited Stephen's children's school. It was one specifically for children of soldiers and police officers. Both of these occupations are low paying and they spend months away from their families. The reward given to them is an education to their children. I also presented them with a small monetary gift for their father's love for the twelve.

When we arrived safely inside of the gates of the guesthouse, I gave everyone a hug. I would not see all of them again until the farewell party Sunday evening. Some of them I would see Sunday morning in the church where we held our seminar a few days earlier. Sarah, Stephen and I exited and went towards guesthouse lobby. Usually, she has the driver take her home. Also, the guards spend the night in the courtyard. Tents with beds were set up outside for them to reside in during our stay here. However, Lawrence requested a meeting with all of the American team leaders, their Ugandan leader associates, and the police officers assigned to their vehicles.

"Well Salongo," Stephen said, "are you pleased with your efforts this week?"

"Very much so," I said. "I have seen more than I could ever explain."

"Luckily," he said, "you won't have to since you were able to have others videotape your program for your wife and children back home."

"This is quite true. I will have to review all these tapes when I get home."

"Will you be joining us next year?" he asked.

"Well, if you promise not to serve too much matoke."

He laughed as he moved on ahead of us, but Sarah was surprisingly silent. I noticed a huge change in her behavior that morning. I did not know exactly what the problem was. I thought it may have been too personal to ask. The culture that I come from is very open and frank. We must be sensitive to the cultures and norms of others. Respect and trust for one another can only be achieved in this manner. I did not want to offend her in any way, since we had been getting along so marvelously this past week. People are entitled to their privacy.

"So Sarah," I said, "what's wrong?"

"Why do you ask?" she replied.

"I noticed that you have been a little down or sad today. Is there any thing that I am able to do?"

"Well, I don't think you can."

"Try me. You never know how a person can help."

"Alright, I will make you a promise."

"Okay."

"After this meeting with Lawrence, if you still want to know, I will tell you. Is that acceptable?"

"Very much so. In America, when one of us hurt, we all hurt. The American way is to always do what you can to help another person in need."

"That is also the Christian way of life."

"Alright. Somehow, I knew you would turn this into a *Bible* study. But, this is good. I have learned so much about myself and others this week."

When we arrived in the lobby, there were names on the tables of the various ministries from the entire team. I noticed Stephen sitting at the table labeled "Children's Ministry." He beckoned us to come join him. Sarah and I sat on either side of him at the table. He was drinking from a bottle of Mango Tango. I got up and retrieved a bottle of water. I put a pack of lemonade in it. I have no use for water except to bathe in it. The only way I could continuously drink water was if it were flavored.

I noticed that the table to the prison ministry was empty. These guys visited prisons throughout the area. I was told that the prisons were deplorable. I asked Stephen about them. Before he was a police officer, he was a prison guard.

"Stephen," I asked, "what are the prisons like around here?"

"Well, we have more of what you would call prison farms. Many of them are just enclosed brick walls with barely anything inside. During the rainy season, all of it falls on the prisoners and the guards. There is a place for the prisoners to use the latrine and a guard office. Most of them sleep on the ground or on a mat, if their families brought them one."

"What about their clothing and shoes?"

"If their families did not bring it to them, they do not have it. Most of them only have the clothes and shoes they came in with at the time of their imprisonment. They are given one meal a day. To receive this meal, they must come on their knees."

"Is the food any good?"

"What do you think?"

"I can only imagine."

"If their families bring them something is there any guarantee that they will get it? I asked this because I know how tempting it can be to take something from someone who has no one to constantly check on them."

"Well, just like any place in the world. There is corruption among the guards and prisoners. As you said, a temptation exists for guards (who receive very little pay) to take something from the prisoners. They do not get paid as much as we do and live in very bad conditions."

"Yes. I remember the prison ministry team telling us that in a meeting."

"A few years ago when your group brought shoes and clothing for them, this became an issue for the guards. The next year, uniforms and shoes were brought for the guards, and they were very happy. They also brought board games and a weekly *Bible* study."

"Do the guards carry guns?"

"Some do, but most do not. If you hurt a guard or try to escape, the consequences are very, very bad."

I could only imagine what they would be. Lawrence stood up and was ready to begin the meeting.

"Welcome back everyone," Lawrence said.

"It must be hard stuck in the guesthouse all day drinking cold water. What do you say Lawrence?" Ray said.

Everyone laughed. We all knew that Lawrence was one of the hardest working persons in the group. He had to coordinate events, monitor each team over the course of two weeks, and constantly worry about our safety. If he received two hours of sleep each night, I would be surprised.

"I'll let that go mate," he replied looking down over his dusty worn-out sunglasses. "I have invited everyone here today to begin a new program. Many of you have been working with the person next to you for days, months, and years."

"Too long," someone shouted from the audience.

"Well," he continued, "I want you to really get to know that person. Everyone who is willing and able is asked to spend one complete 24 hour period with their Ugandan host."

All of the Ugandan members in the group stood up and gave us an applause. The looks on our faces were of astonishment. We were completely speechless. Carol's group (of course) hugged Dr. Rachel, a Ugandan doctor working with the team. Although each of these Ugandan team members live in a home. Some go from livable to "bring the front door over here; it's the dinner table." I later found out that Dr. Rachel had a nice ranch style home complete with running water, television VCR combination and one live-in servant. Although her home would be considered at the poverty level in America to barely lower middle class, it was the Grand Beverly Hills Hotel of Hoima.

"For your safety, a police officer will be staying with you as well," Lawrence continued.

"When will this exchange take place?" Ken asked.

"Right now," he replied. "Have a good evening, and we will see you tomorrow night. I know some of you will be coming back at different times. The prison ministry team will stay at one of the homes located near the prison. So, we won't see them until tomorrow night."

"Can we retrieve a few items from our rooms?" I asked.

"Yes," he replied. "But first, I would like to let the police officers and our Ugandan hosts go to prepare for your departure."

The guards and the Ugandans left the lobby. Some of them were hugging their American counterparts.

"I will meet you at our van," Sarah replied.

"I look forward to talking with you," I said. "I haven't forgotten."

She smiled and walked out of the guesthouse with Stephen.

"We also prepared your place for the evening at your various homes," Ivan stated. "There is a bag in the room in which you will be sleeping. Inside of it are a few items that you will need. There is insect repellent spray that you will spray around the area you will be sleeping. Two new mosquito nets have been provided. Please check immediately for defects. When you leave, you will give your family these nets to keep."

"That's wonderful," Carol said.

"No one will be sleeping on the ground," Ivan added. You have a bed and a new pneumatic mattress. We shipped the mattresses here in the cargo freight we sent months ago. Also, your guard will take a case of water for you. Every host knows the cooking procedures and the food will be safe for you to eat."

"Can they keep the mattress and unused water as well?" Ken asked.

"I suppose we can offer this to them as a gift for hosting us," Lawrence replied. "My wife and I will be staying at the palace with the king."

Ordinarily, the room would have filled with rumblings of murmur at the thought of the leader in a palace, while we were sleeping in the poorest parts of town. However, if you saw the palace where the king in this area lived, the average American would have traded one night in a one star motel. Still, those who are willing to open their mind to new ideas and experiences would have not traded this opportunity for a night at the White House in the Lincoln bedroom.

"Please go to your room and get your sleeping gear and other items that you may need for this evening," Ivan said. "Once again, have a safe evening."

I went to my room to retrieve survival items for the evening. I had a gym bag in which I planned to place various items I purchased while in Africa. I packed my toiletries, flashlights, a set of new clothing, and a few snacks. On our way to one of the schools, Sarah drove me past her home to briefly meet her family. She lived in a safe part of town, and there would not be too much concern. Not surprisingly, LRA members were seen less than twenty miles in the area. However, this is a great distance on foot in the African heat as well as the dangers that lay wait in the bush.

I did not seem to have cause for concern, but it is always good to be vigilant in uncertain surroundings. Even though Ivan said there would be a case of water provided for us, I still took a few bottles, just in case. I never thought I would ever have wished to stay in the discomforts of this room. It would seem like a condominium compared to where I was going in the eyes of some. Yet, I felt that this experience would be one that would impact my life forever.

When I returned to the van, I saw something that I had never seen before. Stephen was sitting in the back talking to Sarah. Abraham, our driver that week, was completely turned around in his chair facing the two of them. As I got closer to the vehicle, I noticed that they were speaking in Bunyuro and I could not understand them. However, I did understand that the tears that fell from Sarah's eyes were of sorrow and not joy.

They did not become aware of me as I approached more closely. I made my presence known by clearing my throat. Abraham immediately smiled at me and started the van. Stephen exited and sat in the front seat. It appeared that everyone knew what was going on except me.

"Okay Sarah," I said, "it's time to tell me what is going on."

"I don't want to burden you with my family problems," she replied.

"Sarah, you are my friend. Remember what you said about Christians helping one another. Now is the time to tell me. If I can't help you, then I'll tell you."

"It's my younger cousin. He has been taken with others."

"Your cousin was taken with whom?"

143

"The LRA soldiers have taken him and other children at his school."

"I don't understand. What do you mean?"

"My mother's sister has only one child. He was sent to a boarding school about 56 kilometers from here. It is not uncommon for LRA soldiers who have been separated from their group to raid homes and schools searching for food and other items. They kill all the witnesses. Sometimes, they take children with them."

"What do they do with the children?"

"They make the girls slaves. They cook and clean for them. All of them are raped multiple times by men who probably have AIDS."

"What about the boys?"

"They make them rape the girls as well. They brainwash them through means of torture. They abuse them and turn them into killing machines. The boys later attack and raid villages with the main army. They also ambush vehicles and travelers as they walk along the roads. They perform most of these evil deeds under the cover of night."

"This is horrible. What do the police do?"

"Well is very difficult to catch them," Stephen replied.

"Why is that?" I asked.

"They are very mobile. Many of them cross the boarders into Sudan or the Congo."

"Are the police permitted to go after them?"

"Not usually, but Ugandan soldiers have snipers that follow them across the boarders. But, this is very very dangerous. The soldiers can be ambushed and killed."

"There are many places for them to hide," Sarah added. "Some hide in Murchison Falls National Park. It is located near the West Nile."

"When I was talking to Ivan one day about the dangers in Uganda, he mentioned that tourists were killed there not too long ago."

"Yes," Stephen said. "It is a very dangerous place at night. However, I am told that this is where they sometimes bring those who have been recently taken prisoner."

"Where is Murchison Falls National Park?"

"It is located northeast of here in a town called Masindi," Steven said. "It will take us less than one hour to travel where we need to go."

"Has anyone ever escaped?"

"Very few have made it out alive. Those who have made it out have contracted AIDS or suffer from lifelong physical problems due to torture. If one of the women escapes, the others are beaten severely. If the woman who escapes is caught, she is brought back to the camp. There, the other women must beat her to death with rods and rocks. Cord wood is placed around her body, and she is burned to ashes, while the other women watch in horror."

After a short period of time, we arrived at Sarah's home. Abraham promptly exited the van and opened the side door for us. When I stepped inside her home, her mother, Theopista, and father, David, were sitting on the couch located in the main living area. Sitting in between them was a woman in tears. She was being comforted by hugs from Ester and rubs on the back by David. I assumed that she was the aunt whose child was abducted by LRA soldiers. There older son Geoffrey was sitting on a wooden chair across from them.

When they noticed me, immediately, David and Theopista came to greet me into their home. Although they were experiencing a horrendous family crisis, African custom would not let my presence go unnoticed. Theopista knelt on the floor in front of me, which always made me uncomfortable. However, this was the custom of older African women and girls when they met clergy and guests of honor. Occasionally, I noticed women of other ages do this as well whenever Sarah and I would walk into a room.

After I accepted David's hand of friendship, I immediately walked towards the aunt. At this point, she too was on her knees. I gently lifted her up and gave her a brief embrace.

"I have heard about your loss," I said. "I pray that God will return your son. What is his name?"

"Ruben," she replied. "I am called Grace."

"Well, may God's grace be upon you through this time."

I turned to David and placed my hand on his shoulder.

"David," I said, "I do not think that this is a good time for me to be here. Maybe we can schedule this overnight visit for another time?"

"Father, we cannot afford to take that risk," Geoffrey said.

"Silence, my son," replied David. "We have a guest in our home."

"What risk David?" I asked. "What is he talking about?"

"Joshua, you have become like a son to me. I have enjoyed reading your letters to our family this past year. Now that you have come to visit us, I truly believe you are a part of our family. But the matter is too dangerous for you to get involved."

"Joshua, we are planning a child rescue," Geoffrey said.

"What is that?" I asked.

"Well, I guess you should know, since your being here will make it possible," replied David. "Come let us allow these angels of mercy to prepare for this evening's meal. I don't want them to be involved or worried more than they are already are right now."

"I will take your bags to your room," Theopista said with a smile.

"Thank you very much for inviting me into your home."

Theopista, Sarah, and Grace went into Geoffrey's room with my bags and closed the curtain behind them. Once they were in there, they began to sing songs of praise. It became somewhat comforting to hear. I had come to the conclusion that everyone in Africa could sing very well. It didn't matter their age or gender, they all appeared to have this innate gift.

"Tell me more about this child rescue," I asked.

"Joshua," Geoffrey said, "the less you know the better."

"Do you trust me my friend?" I asked.

"Very much so," he replied.

"Then, please share. I give you my word that I will not do anything to tear down your plans."

We all sat down in the main living area. David, Geoffrey, Abraham, Stephen and myself. All of us faced Abraham as he went over his plans to rescue Ruben from the ruthless hands of the LRA.

"You see Joshua," he said, "we are tired of the senseless violence of the LRA. They destroy or land, create havoc with our government, and kill innocent people. They actively seek children to fight their war. These children are sexually abused by the soldiers. They are tortured or killed if they refuse to follow the orders of the leaders. They are made into killing machines."

"What is the Ugandan government doing about saving these children?"

"Unfortunately, these children may be killed in a firefight with Ugandan soldiers or police officers. They don't know that the people shooting at them are children. These children are lifelong victims. If they are captured, they may have to face prosecution for the atrocities they committed. They may have brought shame to their family or village through what was done to them or what they participated in while in captivity. But they all will suffer emotional pain the rest of their lives."

"How are the people of Uganda helping them?"

"We are quite an understanding people. We understand the anguish the girls will suffer if they return. They may never marry or live a customary life. The boys who have committed atrocities have to complete a ritual of cleansing. Then, they will be accepted back into their communities. However, as with the girls, they have lifelong scars and no one really to counsel them properly back to health."

"We will not allow that to happen to our family member!" Geoffrey said.

"Calm down," David said, "that anger of yours will not prove useful on this mission."

"Forgive me father," he replied, "but I love Ruben so much."

"We all do my son."

David looked at Geoffrey as to reassure him. Geoffrey appeared to be calmed by this and sat down on the floor.

"Joshua," Stephen said, "I must be totally honest with you."

"I never thought you were not," I said.

"I am married to Sarah's sister. Her name is Dorcus." he said.

I was shocked for a brief moment. Then, I answered him.

"I do not think this was dishonest."

"Well, that is why I requested to be with the children's ministry during these next couple of weeks. I wanted to make sure that nothing would happen to my sister-in-law."

"What could happen?"

"Europeans and Americans make good targets for terrorists. They know that they will appear in the news if they kill one. So, when I heard that Sarah would be working with an American this week, I asked my Lieutenant could I work with your team. He did not know that I was related to Sarah either. If he had, he probably would not have allowed me to do so."

"I would have probably done the same thing if I were in your position."

I turned to Abraham. "What is your role in this?"

"Geoffrey and I have been friends for many years," Abraham said.

"Yes. Yes, we have." Geoffrey replied.

"But, this family has been a greater friend to me," Abraham replied. "When I needed financial help to get my license, Geoffrey convinced his father to loan me the money to pay for my school fees."

"And you have paid us back my son already," David said.

"I know you have," he replied. "But, I want to do what I can. My vehicle is at your disposal."

"You are most kind," David said.

"Thank you my friend," Geoffrey whispered looking at Abraham with a smile.

"What can I do to help?" I asked.

"You can stay here and be in prayer for our mission." Abraham said. "It is much too dangerous for you out there. You do not know the land."

"I have been on many military operations in the United States Army. Possibly, I can be. . . ."

"Here in Africa," David said, "the rules of war are quite different."

The curtain from Geoffrey's bedroom opened.

"Excuse me sirs," Theopista said.

Everyone in the room stood up to acknowledge her presence.

"But we must prepare for our guest and evening meal," she said. "Please excuse us."

"Yes please," David said.

Sarah and Grace followed her outside their home.

"May I ask what your plan is?" I asked.

"It is very simple," Stephen said. "The four of us will drive to the area around Murchison Falls National Park. Abraham will park the van a few hundred yards in the bush from the entrance of the park. Geoffrey, Abraham, and I will go to the location where we believe that the children are being held."

"Once we find out where they are, I will separate from the group and create a diversion," David said.

"What is it?" I asked.

"I have two flares I will light. I will attempt to lure the soldiers away from the children and in the opposite direction of the van. I also have a weapon. I will fire shots into the air. This will definitely draw them in my direction."

"Once they investigate or confusion has been created, we will go in and rescue Ruben," Stephen said.

"But how will you see this in the dark night?" I asked.

"It is much too dangerous to travel in the night," he replied. We plan to do this at dusk. This is when they are most vulnerable."

"I will be waiting for them in the van to pick them up. I will then meet David a little further down the road heading towards home. The LRA does not like to be seen in the daylight for fear of government soldiers and police officers," Stephen said.

"Most likely, they will only chase us as far as the road, if they chase us at all," Abraham said. "Everyone will have a weapon. I trust we do not have to use them."

"But we will if we have too," Geoffrey stated as he pulled his hand gun out and cocked it.

"Put that away!" David said. "There is no need for that now."

"Is there another way?" I asked.

"There is no other way," Geoffrey replied. "If we report this incident to the authorities, they will only take a report.

The longer we wait, the more difficult it will be to rescue Ruben."

"If he is still alive," Abraham said.

"He is," Geoffrey said. "And we will not believe differently until we are sure!"

"Of course," Abraham said. "I am sorry."

"No, my friend," Geoffrey said. "It is I who am sorry. I am trying to control myself. But, this entire situation upsets me very much."

"We must move quickly," Stephen said. "It is our only hope. If we don't rescue Rueben, I fear that every time I am in a firefight with the LRA I may either kill him, or he will be forced to kill me."

The room immediately became silent as everyone contemplated that thought. From that moment on, until the evening meal, the subject was never brought up again. This would be my first night with an African family. I anticipated what it would be like.

was happening so quickly. What was once the thought in someone's mind had now become my reality – our reality.

That evening, we gathered about a table set in the middle of the living area. On it were covered pots and bowls that contained the evening meal. David invited everyone to join hands in a circle, and we sang a song and prayed over our supper. It was an African feast that most Americans would have called a light lunch. I later learned from Abraham that the chicken that was being served was their only one. Sarah knew I would have never allowed her mother to kill that chicken for my benefit. However, if I did not eat a little something, I remembered that it would be a major insult to the family. Each swallow was both flavorful and dreadful to my taste buds and conscience.

I noticed that David did not eat that much. This was commented on by both his wife and son. They knew something was wrong.

"I am okay," Abraham said. "I just need to lie down for a few minutes. You will please excuse me."

Everyone, except me, looked at each other with a knowing glance. I noticed that he had begun to sweat a little more as the evening progressed. At first, I assumed that this was due to his age and the climate. However, the others and I had not experienced the same symptoms.

"Let me help you," Theopista said.

"Ah. Theopista, my dear wife. Thank you very much."

He placed his arm around her shoulders, and they walked into their bedroom. His light twitching earlier that evening had given way to noticeable shaking.

"What will we do now?" Geoffrey asked.

"What can we do?" Steven said.

"My father is no condition to go with us."

"It would appear that he has early stages of the fever," Abraham said.

"The fever. What's that?" I asked.

"My father contracted malaria," Sarah said. "We don't have the money to buy the medication to keep it under control. Once or twice a year, he has these episodes of shaking and a high fever."

"I know that the medical team brought pills," I said. "Right now, you will go back to the guesthouse. Have them contact Ivan. He will know exactly where the nurses can be reached. I am sure we can help you."

"No," David said as his head poked out from the bedroom curtain. "I will not allow it. You will do no such thing. It will compromise our plans."

"But father, your health," Sarah said in a cracked voice.

"I have lived this long with the fever my dear," he said. "I have no fears. If you alert anyone to come here, they will stay here all night. It is okay. Just allow me to rest."

He began to cough. You could notice the discoloration in his face. Sarah went to the bedroom with a bowl of water. Grace followed her with a towel.

The men's looks at the table were in utter despair. Although David was not the main participant in their plans, he was a key element. It was as if everything they worked for had now been crushed.

"We still may be able to do it," Geoffrey held.

"No," Stephen said, "it will be too dangerous. We need someone to create a diversion."

"Maybe I can do the distraction as well," Abraham stated.

"No. We need you to prepare the vehicle."

"Then I'll create the diversion," Geoffrey said.

"It is not possible," Stephen said. "I need your extra set of eyes. Also, we are the only two who know exactly what Rueben looks like."

"What will we do?" Abraham said.

No one spoke for a time. You could hear the moaning coming from the back bedroom. No one made eye contact with anyone in the room. It was quite evident that it was over. It appeared as if Grace would lose her son to a rouge army. These were men who neither regarded his family or even his very life. Grace would have to live the remainder of her days in Hoima wondering if her son were dead or alive until her death.

"There is one possible solution," I said.

No said anything, but they all knew what I was thinking.

"It is too much to ask," Stephen said. "You have a family waiting for you back in America."

"We want to send you back alive," Abraham said.

"I can do this," I said. "I know how to use a weapon, and I am familiar with that area a little."

"What do you mean?" asked Geoffrey.

"There is a school not to far from the entrance of the park," I said.

"Walyoba," Stephen said. "That's correct. We were there on Wednesday."

"Yes," I answered.

"That is the school Ruben was taken from," Geoffrey stated.

"I am in excellent physical condition. If something happens, I can go and hide there and wait for you. You said they don't like to be exposed in the day. Maybe they won't return to the place where they kidnapped the children."

"I think he can do it," Abraham said.

"I'm sure he can," Stephen replied. "But the risks are just too great."

"I am quite aware of the risk," I said.

"Can you light a flare?" Stephen asked.

"It does not sound too difficult," I said. "Do you have one here?"

"I have two," he replied. "One was a back-up just in case David needed it. Abraham, go to your van and get a flare."

Abraham got up from the table and headed out the door. Within the span of a minute or two, he returned with a road flare.

"I know how to use this," I said. "It will be a piece of cake."

"What do you mean cake," Geoffrey said.

"I mean it will be easy."

"Then, let us take our sleep," Stephen said. "Abraham, place these back in the bag. We will leave in seven hours."

Well, here we are right now. Everything up until this point was past memories, I recalled on the silent drive up to Masindi. I remembered all these events from packing my clothes at home to last night when I agreed to go on this mission of mercy. Here we sit, a few yards from the entrance of Murchinson Falls. This is no memory, but life as it is now in real time. It is still dark, and the sun has yet to make its ascension. We had to drive slowly and without headlights for almost a half of a mile. Stephen was sure that their might be LRA scouts in the area.

I wrote my wife and children a letter and placed it on mattress back in Geoffrey's room. It was not a long letter. I had to be prepared for anything. Of course, I told my wife and daughters how much I loved them. I explained to Precious that if we were in the same situation, I know these brave men would do the same for us. Most importantly, I told my son that on this road of life, we may be called to give the ultimate sacrifice – our lives for others.

Was I really prepared to do this task? Less than a year ago my biggest concern was whether or not Tony Dungee could take the Colts all the way to the big dance this time. This seemed so trite right now. My life could end at any moment. I was well out of the arch of safety of the United

States borders. Possibly, someone else should have been sitting where I am now.

However, as Harriet Tubman could not single handedly liberate every single slave, I could not rescue each child in that camp. Nevertheless, as she was born to be the great emancipator of her day, I was born for such a time as this. Harriet fearlessly faced the rope of the bounty hunter. I was presently prepared to face the machete of the LRA solider. Doubt was replaced with assurance. Most importantly, strength and courage were the only emotions I could feel that very second. My e-mail name said it all, "Joshuaone9". I would be strong and courageous.

"Let's go," Stephen said.

"May God go with you my brother," Abraham remarked.

"He will," I said. "If I don't see you in a few minutes, I'll see you in eternity."

I quietly closed the van door and walked up the dark dusty road. Once I had gone about a tenth of a mile, I had to walk about 50 yards directly into the bush. My night vision seemed fair that morning, and I was not sure that I could remember any of the land marks back to the road. Every tree and bush looks the same in Africa. A minute red line was beginning to form on the horizon to my left. That was the best landmark of all. My destiny was in the hands of the sun.

I did not put any repellent on. I was aware that experienced LRA soldiers who had been in the bush for quite some time could smell its scent and possibly give my position away. Bite after bite, I was hopeful that the insects feasting on my body were not from the West Nile River, which was directly right of my current position.

I was to give Stephen and Geoffrey a few minutes to get into position. They gave me Sarah's cell phone. It was placed on vibrate. Once they were in position, they would call me to initiate the first flare. This would be the most important call of my life. If they were caught, possibly they would be tutored and forced to tell of our plans. This would compromise the safety of Abraham and me. Sitting crouched in the bushes was probably the most extreme form of call waiting I could imagine.

I made a clearing to place the flare; I did not want to have an out of control fire torch a national treasure. Nor did I want to be involved in an international incident. I checked the time on my watch. It had been almost five minutes. I wondered if something had gone wrong. I thought it would be best for me to head back to the road or school.

A few minutes passed, and the phone vibrated. That was the signal. I pulled a flare from my backpack and lit it. I began to fire shots in the air with my gun and scream like the biggest Mandinka in the Congo on his way to meet his bride. It was not soon after that that I began to draw fire. A hail of bullets whistled through the treetops above my head. I did not know, or care, if the bullets came from an individual or army.

I headed for the road. The sun began to slowly rise and eventually triumphantly overtake the northern Ugandan horizon. I tripped over the biggest and softest log I ever had in my life. From its movement, I immediately learned that it was a black poisonous snake. It raised its head. It was not fully awakened and was somewhat groggy. I noticed a huge lump inside its body, and I slowly moved away. I did not know who or what it was, but I got up and ran towards the road as it turned in my direction exposing its fangs. I honestly believe that if Kunta Kentay had run through the bush like I did that day, he would have never met Chicken George.

Out of the bush and down the road I ran. I was screaming, crying, and breathing heavily. I threw my gun in the direction of the snake. It was not my finest hour. Of all the days I could die, it wasn't going to be today, if I could help it. More intense gunfire was going towards the direction of the van, which was exactly where I was headed.

When I reached the van, Abraham was waving me towards him. I went to greet him, and he pushed me down to the ground. Simultaneously, both he and the LRA soldier (who was aiming at me) fired their weapons. They both were killed instantly.

Bullets were now hitting the back of the van. Men and children were coming out of the bush with weapons drawn. Some of them were totally naked, but well endowed with weapons. I got into the van and could not find the key. They were in Abraham's top pocket, where I noticed him place them many times. I jumped out of the van and rolled him over. Still under fire, I retrieved the keys. The engine would not start. It was then that I learned that it was a stick shift, and I had flooded the engine.

Screaming and yelling, the soldiers drew closer. I don't know if it were them screaming louder or I. The seven hundred dollar 1990 Subaru that I bought years ago in Clarksville, Tennessee with a stick shift seemed like the greatest bargain of my life. I put the stick in neutral and started the engine. I stomped down on the clutch and put the van into second gear. With a jerk and spinning tires, I was headed down the road at break neck speed. The odometer was on forty before I shifted to the third gear.

Waving me down along the road was Stephen. He had a child straddled along his back. I didn't see Geoffrey anywhere in sight.

"Get in," I said. "Where's Geoffrey?"

"I don't know," he replied. "One of the soldiers surprised us. He alerted the others, and we had to separate."

Pointing at the child, "Put him in the back," I said.

"Is he Rueben?"

"Yes. This is my nephew."

The child was somewhat dazed, but alive. I noticed that he had been beaten across his back, which had exposed wounds.

"Where's Abraham?"

"He didn't make it."

"What?"

"He's dead."

In an instant, his face went from despair to anger.

"I'm going back for Geoffrey."

"You don't have to Stephen."

"Yes I do."

"No you don't. Look."

As Stephen turned around, he could see Geoffrey coming down the road with three girls. One of them was in his arms. He put her down, and she ran towards the van. An older girl was shot and fell to the ground. Geoffrey began to shoot his weapon towards the bush. The first girl who made it to the van was crying uncontrollably. She latched onto Stephen and would not let him go. The second girl climbed inside and crawled into a fetal position and lay on the floor covering her head. Geoffrey made it closer to the van. Only yards away, he was shot.

"Joshua, come back!" Stephen shouted.

Without regard for myself, I ran out of the van toward his direction.

"Joshua, come back!"

When I reached Geoffrey, he did not respond when I called his name. I ran rapidly back to the van. I opened the back door of the van. I lifted him into the van as a hail of bullets flew around and through the van. He simply said "yes." Stephen moved the girl from him and got into the driver's seat. Without even knowing if we were securely in, he took off down the road. I fell out the back of the van, which was heading down the road. It stopped, and I ran towards it, while the shooting continued.

A man ran out of the bush and came towards me. He had his machete drawn and was prepared to come down with it on my body. A boy soldier with a weapon pointed at me came from out of the bush as well. He cocked his weapon and fired several times. He killed the man with the machete. I stood there and looked at him in amazement.

"You go home," he said. "Now!"

I made it to the van and jumped in. When I turned around, I did not see the boy in the bush. However, the soldier lay dead on the road. By this time, it was clearly daylight. Our gamble that they would not come after us paid off. I don't know who that boy was, but he saved my life. If his skin were three shades lighter, he would look exactly like my son. Someone would say that hysterics had taken over my mind. Was there a boy or a very young man that appeared on the road to assist me?

On the drive back, we learned that both of the girls had been abducted the same day as Ruben. Luckily, neither one of them had been raped. However, they were beaten severely. We made it back safely to Sarah's home. We sounded the horn as we neared Sarah's home. The neighbors and others came running outside.

"Grace," Stephen said, "come outside."

The door of the humble home flew open, and she emerged. She flung open the door and began to embrace her son. The blood from his body that now was on her clothes did not seem to matter.

"Easy now," Geoffrey said, "you are going to hurt the boy."

"Oh no," she said looking at her nephew, "Geoffrey, you are hurt. Theopista, Sarah come quickly. Geoffrey is hurt."

Immediately, they came outside.

"I am okay," he said. "I just have a little wound in my side."

{}

"Let us come inside and dress these wounds," Theopista said.

"Who are these lovely ladies?" Sarah asked.

"We rescued them from the soldiers as well," he said.

"Come," she said, "you are most welcome."

Before Sarah went into the house, she handed me my letter.

"I was waiting to give this to you in person," she said. "I had no intentions of mailing it. I knew you would return to us."

She pulled my face to her lips and kissed me on the check.

"Thank-you."

I learned of another tragedy standing there with Sarah. Unfortunately, David did not know that we made it back safely. Theopista told us that just before he died, he called for his son to go home. He touched his side and died with a smile on his face. Geoffrey was wounded in his side and he did not respond to me when I initially came upon him. I wondered if there was a connection.

My road did not end in Hoima. While on that road, I met a courageous man who gave the ultimate sacrifice – his life in exchange for another who did not deserve or earn it. A husband and father of three, I already knew Precious and the kids would be willing to support his family. Each of the three children would have sponsors for life. We vowed no one on the team would ever learn of this encounter in Uganda. Still, I would never let my children forget a man named Abraham – their Ugandan father, who we all would meet again in eternity.

APPENDIX

After my initial visit to Uganda, I returned three months later alone to train club leaders to be trainers for those persons who were seeking to be ENK-U club leaders. The response was overwhelming. We had to turn back persons wanting to get involved. I wanted to ensure quality training and sincerity of the heart for children's ministry. The following is a letter sent by Lydia 12 months after initial training/visit.

We give glory to God for how the Lord has brought us. From 81 clubs, we now have 126 clubs in total number. All these clubs are in different parts/churches of Hoima, Masindi and Kibaale districts. It is our plan by the end of this year to raise the number to 200 clubs.

In addition, participants were encouraged to advocate for children's ministry in their locality, since it is one of the neglected ministries. This will help us to raise future leaders who are God fearing.

As a way of encouraging ENK-U club leaders, certificates and clothes were given to club-leaders who have been doing good work for the last eight (8) months to motivate them and encourage others also to do likewise.

In addition, new participants were awarded certificates, teaching materials like bibles, bible pictures, balls, transport refund to mention a few.

There was participation of both club leaders and trainers. Many topics were handled by different facilitators and participants appreciated in their evaluation that it was so good and encouraging.

Further more school visits were also successful. We give thanks to the Almighty God for his work through his servant Dr. Therone Wade and the school Team ministry because 600 kids/children came to the Lord and we prayed for them and were handed over to their school chaplains/patrons.

Yours in Christ
Rev. Lydia

The following are excerpts of letters from ENK-U club leaders regarding the schools, trainings, and ENK-U clubs.

Dear Sir:

First and foremost, I thank God almighty for the vision of children evangelism ministry (Proverbs 22:6) in which we have been called to serve in response to the Great Commission. From this training, it has become clearer to me and I feel challenged to reach out to children more than before.

I have gained more skills on how to share the gospel with the children. . . by reference in using environmental colours that may help to present the message.

Through this training, I have also discovered that simple games are necessary before sharing the gospel as a way of attracting the children's attention.

I addition, I have not been limiting the gospel to our ENK-U club only. It was so interesting to see big numbers of children in primary schools from different religions around us turning to our Lord. Through this training, I realized the importance of having a purpose in my ministry – and this is none other but glorifying God.

Lastly, I want to state it clearly that the gospel was full of grace and practical love. It's my prayer that we are to uphold the vision to bless others too. Otherwise, I can't thank you enough. May God abundantly bless you Therone and the team.

Live Long – Come Again.

Yours faithfully,
FB

Dear Sir:

Thank you for the training. It was good on my behalf and it really helped me and my club at large. My club is doing well and many children have turned to God, because of the training I received from you. God bless you.

I learned how to prepare myself before teaching the children. Also, how to win children for the kingdom of God and even how can children serve God. Now, my club is hot for Jesus. There are over 80 children. Please, keep up with that spirit.

My club grew because I used the knowledge I got from the training I had. It is the cry of my heart that when you come back, please come and visit my club and I will be happy. The children are winning more children for Christ and bringing them to my club. I really thank the Lord so much for what you are doing and for that vision. May He give you more wisdom and bless you more abundantly above all. Me He keep you in His fearing until you reach heaven and jubilant with Him.

I remain
AJ

Praise God.

Thank you for the <u>Children's Resource Bible</u>. Thank you for the training. It helped me a lot. The visit to our school was very exciting in that all the members of staff and children were welcoming and eager to hear the Word. They were happy to receive the gifts from our visitors.

Certainly, my ENK-U club "Lord's Club" grew bigger. Since then and the attendance has been good. God has helped us to create friendships with our neighbors through our club and we continue praising HIM AMEN.

RM
"Lord's Club"

Brother in Christ

I would like to thank you so much for everything you have done, especially for the prayer you pray for our clubs. I will be happy to see you again. I am looking forward for another training. Let's pray for it. Since our training, I have seen some changes in my *Bible* classes and to enjoy it more. My club has grown. My children visit the elderly singing songs to them and praying for them. Plus do some work like cleaning their home.

I remain
Ms. MT

Dear Sir:

Greetings to you in the mighty name of Jesus Christ. Praise, glory, and honor be to the living God who has enabled me to make this report. I want to thank God for the training. I was so good. The training helped me as a teacher how to start a good conversation in order to share the gospel using the materials and to capture a child's attention and giving chance to a child to receive Christ.

After the school visits, new children are coming to join the club and other people are having a desire to start home *Bible* study in their homes. So far, God has enabled me to disciple one already. She has started.

On behalf of my ENK-U club (New Life Club), children are thankful for the gifts you gave them. I taught them how to share the Good News in the simple way using the bracelet and I gave to each child. Now they are able to share with their fellow friends in their neighborhood and even at school.

Really, you people have been a blessing to me. The materials you gave me has made the work easier than before. I have learned many things, such as preparing a *Bible* lesson, leading a child to Christ, and much more.

Thank you for remembering us individually in your prayers.

From
DK

Dear Salongo:

I had nothing concerning any knowledge about the children, but when I attended the training I am perfect now. Your schedule did not allow us to be blessed by a visit from you. But, I know that it was God's plan that we were not ready enough and now we look forward to meet you anytime you come back.

My club is still growing and since that, it has many different children from different homes in that they're not equally dressed. So others feel small when we gather.

In my neighborhood I have no other club next to mine. The parents of the children I teach they're appreciating because their children have changed from behaving badly to behaving nicely in that I have been given responsibility to groom 15yrs and 16 yrs old boys in our neighborhood. I will ask you kindly to help with anything you think can give a hand to their coming up. We look forward to receiving you back in Uganda.

Yours in Christ
NMP

Dear Brother:

With much happiness you will allow me to take this opportunity to thank you for whatever you are doing. We have a very good number of children which is between 110-129 children. We need to share ideas in order to make our clubs better. In addition that God is truly using us to do a good work because children are accepting Jesus Christ as their personal Saviour.

May God continue to bless you.

Yours in the service,
FRB

Because of the training, one club leader was asked to travel outside her country to provide training to her neighboring African sisters and brothers.

Although we visited mainly primary (elementary) schools, we did manage to visit a couple of high schools. Below is a letter from one of the children I met.

Dear Mr. Therone,

How are you and how is God's work going on? Back to me I am fine and going on with God as my personal Savior. I have written this letter to appreciate for the gift of a Holy chain you left for me these ends and to inform you that I was so grateful to keep on praying for your family. I have done this since you left and I have kept on thanking God for the gift of praying He gave to me. Also, for choosing me as my friend.

I am a God fearing child and always I consider Him as my just priority in whatsoever I do. Since I started praying for your family, I have never regretted why I do it. I love praying and preaching too. By God's mercy, I am working hard in my studies in order to succeed and do his work and service.

I was so grateful to receiving news that you were coming these ends again. I would be happy if I saw you coming to meet me and tell me about Therone Jr., Christa, and Naomi. How are they? I love them so much though we have never met. The *Bible* tells us to believe without seeing. How is your dear wife? I hope God is giving them a lot of blessings. I promise to continue pray for them and loving them as long as I live.

May God be with you always and may He bless your family as well. May He reward you for your good work.

Best regards to your family, relatives, and friends.

Yours Sincerely,
KS

The following is a list of the top ten prayer concerns from club leaders:

1. Hundreds of children are displaced from their families and living alone in open fields.
2. Children are being sexually defiled sometimes by neighbours or relatives.
3. Women are dumping kids into the bush or pit latrines.
4. There is child sacrifice.
5. Half of the girls who begin school drop out due to pregnancy. (Many cannot continue school after age

12 because not being able to afford sanitary napkins or similar material).

6. The majority of children we meet have been battered.
7. A number of children are malnourished due to poor feeding.
8. The number of HIV/AIDS in children has increased.
9. There is an attack of children through drug abuse.
10. The boys in some schools are being molested.

The following is from a man who was a former orphan helped by the orphan ministry discussed in text. He is now studying at the University.

I am called A. E., 20 years old, male. I was born in 1983 in a village called Kihuukya, Hoima, Uganda. My parents, my father was called E. M. and my mother was called K. S. They are both dead. We are 23 children of same father but different mothers. In 1992 our father passed away because of AIDS and by that time we used to stay with our mother. After some years she also followed him in 1995 by same disease AIDS. From the beginning of 1995, we started to stay with our grandmother who was weak because her legs were broken in 1997.

I remained at school until my grandmother's legs got broken. For some years I went back to school and I finished my primary level and then I joined secondary school level at Mandela Secondary School. I have been staying in the house of Bishop in the village called Kihomboza. They have been helping me with things like clothes, food and others. They also have other people to look after. I completely depend on

God's mercy for my studies. My prayer is that God will provide.

AE

The following letter is from one of the guardians of a sponsored orphan:

I assure you that your love for the people of Bunyoro is felt through your actions extended to all of us. God is using you so mightily in this part of the world. Many sponsored children beam with a smile of hope, as they receive your extended hand of help, and that of all the loving sponsors, who have by faith accepted to give to these needy children.

Many did not have the hope for fees to attend school, but now this hope is restored. Many had never slept on a mattress, but now some have got it. For some of the children getting scholastic material e.g. books, pens, math sets etc was a dream which could not be realized, but now these are provided to them. What a wonderful moment for all these children. It is delight in their hearts. Hope is rekindled. All the sponsors have brightened the dark path of our children.

You have not done all this for the children alone but for the Almighty in Heaven. He will reward each effort you have put a million times. God bless you indeed.

Rev. C.

One sponsored orphan wrote:

"Without your help, I would be a street boy. At first I thought that no hand can be given to me but now it's more than a hand. My appreciation will continue to no end. I wish my late mum could rise and thank you more but impossible. She died of excessive blood loss at the hospital on 5th Jan 2005. When she died we had no rescuer me and young brother. Your love is just beyond passion. This transition will help me to compose a song. Once again may the almighty be with you.

Yours faithfully,
S.

Printed in the United States
111126LV00002B/15/A

9 781604 774931